e you pushing me?"

He couldn't say what he wanted. He only knew what he didn't want. "I don't want you to go. Stay here with me. Let's just see what could happen. Don't we owe ourselves that? A chance at maybe...I don't know...happiness?"

Madeleine crossed her arms over her chest and raised her head as if seeking divine intervention. "That's not going to happen. I still work for you. If you think I'm going to set up house here and be your little lady...so not going to happen."

"You're right. I was stupid. I forgot one last thing."

This time Michael did pounce. He had his hands around her upper arms holding her in place.

"Madeleine, you're fired."

It was the last thing he said before he swooped down and kissed her.

What do you want from me

Dear Reader,

For as long as I can remember I've had a crush on George Stephanopoulos. I think it might be because the name "Steph" appears in his last name. I mean, how cool would it have been to be Steph Stephanopoulos? But beyond the name connection, I was always fascinated by how he was able to rise to the top of the political world so quickly. He was this super boy wonder and many people credit him with making an unknown candidate a president.

The idea of doing a story featuring a character like him appealed to me. Then I thought of another young person involved with the president, who also became a household name, but for a very different reason. That's when it hit me. What if I combined George Stephanopoulos and Monica Lewinsky? What kind of challenges would that create?

My heroine Madeleine Kane is that twisted brainchild and her challenges are many. Good thing she's got a hero like Michael Langdon to help her along. The two of them are pretty messed up, but together they learn that love will help them to take that *One Final Step*.

I love to hear from readers so if you are in the mood you can contact me at www.stephaniedoyle.net.

Enjoy!

Stephanie Doyle

One Final Step

STEPHANIE DOYLE

HARLEQUIN®
entertain, enrich, inspire™

Recycling programs
for this product may
not exist in your area.

ISBN-13: 978-0-373-60734-1

ONE FINAL STEP

Copyright © 2012 by Stephanie Doyle

ABOUT THE AUTHOR

Stephanie Doyle, a dedicated romance reader, began to pen her own romantic adventures at age sixteen. She began submitting to Harlequin Books at age eighteen and by twenty-six, her first book was published. Fifteen years later, she still loves what she does as each book is a new adventure. She lives in South Jersey with two kittens who have taken over everything. When she isn't thinking about escaping to the beach, she's working on her next story idea.

Books by Stephanie Doyle

HARLEQUIN SUPERROMANCE

1773—THE WAY BACK

SILHOUETTE ROMANTIC SUSPENSE

1554—SUSPECT LOVER
1650—THE DOCTOR'S DEADLY AFFAIR

SILHOUETTE BOMBSHELL

36—CALCULATED RISK
52—THE CONTESTANT
116—POSSESSED

Other titles by this author available in ebook format.

For Kimberly and Emil

You may live on the other side of the ocean but family bonds never break.

CHAPTER ONE

MICHAEL LANGDON LOOKED at the woman on the opposite side of his wide desk and felt as if he'd been struck on the head with a bat. Having previously experienced such a sensation, he felt it was an accurate description. But looking at her was far less painful.

She was the most beautiful woman he'd ever seen. He knew in that moment—she was going to change his life.

Then he shook off the ridiculous thoughts. Just as he'd shaken off the effects of actually being hit by the bat. Only, there was still a buzzing in his head and as he took notice of his body, he found himself shifting in his chair and wondering.

"I'm surprised you accepted my invitation," he said.

He watched as her right eyebrow arched, slightly framing a perfectly shaped cobalt-blue eye. The color was everything he'd heard about and read about. And it was more amazing than anything he'd seen on television.

Cobalt-blue eyes combined with dark, long hair that had reddish highlights he suspected were real. Her skin looked as if it would feel silky to the touch and her lips were full enough to make a man think of the things men usually liked to think about when it came to a woman's mouth. Her chin was slightly pointed, a small flaw that prevented her from being a goddess yet at the same time made her that much more intriguing because it meant she was real and not mythical.

"Ben Tyler is a personal friend, as well as my employer. When he asked as my employer, I refused. When he asked as a friend, I had no choice."

Her voice was cool and clipped. Sophisticated and well balanced. Everything an Ivy League education should produce.

"How is Ben doing?"

She turned her head. "Not well."

Michael nodded. He'd known about the cancer, of course, but Ben was one of the toughest fighters he'd ever met. If anyone had a chance of beating it, it was Ben. He would be that one man in a million.

"I called him because I needed the best. Because what I'm about to do is very important. Not for me or my company but for the country. Maybe even the world."

She didn't smirk or look away. A woman like Madeleine Kane understood events that impacted the world.

Michael knew by her silence that he was being invited to make his pitch. It was like being granted permission to speak by the queen. He shifted in his chair again, then placed both elbows on the desk and clasped his hands together.

"I've created something. A car that I believe will revolutionize the industry. I need to convince people it's real and credible and not another Langdon prototype or an interesting anomaly."

"Why do you care what people think? You have an idea…you should build it and sell it."

"I can't do it alone." He sighed. "I wish I could. I don't have the resources the bigger companies do. I don't want this to be a high-end car that only a few can afford. I want to make it available to the masses. For that I need a partner. To get one of those, I need to rebuild my image. It's time to lose the old race-car persona and focus on who I am as an inventor and industry leader."

Madeleine crossed her legs slowly. He couldn't help but let his gaze follow the length of her panty-hose-clad leg to the simple black three-inch pump.

Her ankle was a work of art.

"Did you hear me?"

Michael lifted his gaze.

"I said what you're asking for won't be easy. Your reputation has been very firmly established in the American media as a playboy. Someone who builds fast cars and dates…"

"Fast women?"

"I was going to say well-known actresses. I would never speculate on a woman's sexual proclivities because she happens to be pretty."

No, Michael thought. *You wouldn't.*

"You're known for your flair and style," she continued. "Not for your substance, Mr. Langdon. I'm sorry to be so blunt."

"No, please. It's why I brought you here. I need you to fix me. I need you to help me show my substance to the world—otherwise when I talk about this design to the media they won't listen. I need them to listen. My competitors, other industry leaders, and I suspect maybe even the government, will all want to know the potential of what I have to offer."

"You're talking about an electric car. It's not the first of its kind. You're going to have to give me more than that if you want to convince me."

"More than that? It's not enough that I'm willing to pay you?"

Again the eyebrow rose nearly into the center of her forehead. How did she do that and why did it make him feel half his size?

"I don't need money, Mr. Langdon. The work I do currently for Ben pays my bills sufficiently. You're asking me to remake you. To create a new story for you. Something I haven't done in a long time, but the last time I did do it, that man became president. If you want to convince me to take you on, I'm going to have to believe in what you're doing. More importantly, I'm going to have to believe in you."

Yes, he thought. He wanted that. He wanted this woman to believe in him, although for the life of him he couldn't figure out why that was important.

"Okay, first of all, I'm not talking about *just* an electric car. My design will not only be affordable but will have a much higher sustained energy output, and can be built with the factories we have now. I'm talking about a fully integrated computer that can make real-time driving decisions. I'm talking about no more accidents." He paused for a breath, feeling the excitement he always did when he started talking about his baby.

"Go on."

"I'm talking about a car that can drive itself. And I can do it cheaper than anyone else. Which means bringing a product to the masses within the next two to five years. Other companies trying to accomplish the same thing are projecting seven to ten years. I'm talking about the future, only making that future happen today."

He waited while she considered him for a time. "You are certainly very passionate about this, Mr. Langdon."

"I'm very passionate about a great many things, Ms. Kane."

She didn't like that. He could see it right away in her face. He hadn't intended the sexual innuendo, but it was there, and instantly her body reacted by tightening subtly.

"My project and helping the environment—"

"Partying, women, scandals."

He wasn't going to defend nor explain his behavior. "Look, are you going to take the job or not?"

"We still have more to discuss. First, what do you envision I will do for you?"

Impatiently Michael leaned back in his

chair. It had been a while since he'd been in a position other than complete and total power. Finding himself on the other side of the coin was surprisingly...*uncomfortable.* Yet he needed this woman, so she controlled the shots.

He didn't like it and part of him wanted to escort her contained and cool self to the door. However, the idea of watching her leave didn't sit well with him, either. Which was ridiculous. Of course she had to leave.

"I guess you would do what you do best. Rebuild my image, create a persona the media will respond to, send the message to the world about who I am and what I'm about. Give me direction on how I go about interacting with the public and the media. Isn't that what you did for...*him?*"

Michael shouldn't have added the emphasis on the last word. It had been a jab at her for making him feel weaker than he was. She was already reaching for the briefcase she'd set down next to her chair.

"Sorry," he said before she could stand. "I don't play games. Not in business. You're one of the most talented political handlers in the world. That's why I want you. To remake my image. To get me elected—if not by the people then by my peers, the people who judge me."

"I was a political handler. Now I write position papers for political action committees that contract with the Tyler Group. You don't need a thesis from me. You need someone who would work closely with you to reshape your image. That means event planning, cultivating certain media contacts and any number of other tasks."

"Yes," he agreed. "That can't be you?"

She looked around his office. He knew she saw money in the furniture, in the artwork. Detroit wasn't necessarily a city known for elegance and riches, but it was his home—always had been, even when he lived overseas. When he'd decided to start his own company there wasn't even a question about doing so here, but that didn't mean he was coming back to the Detroit he knew as a kid. His new Detroit was filled with all the things his money could buy.

"You said it wasn't about the money, but I'll pay anything Ben demands," he said. But she already knew that money was not an issue.

No response. It agitated him.

"I'll do everything you say," he offered. "Within reason, of course."

Still he could see her mulling it over in that big brain of hers.

"Not for nothing, but I would think you get sick of writing papers all day. Don't you want to get back to doing what you love? You're a kingmaker, for crying out loud. Not a research-policy wonk."

That played. Her eyes lit up. "Can you give me until tomorrow to consider your offer?"

This time she was asking his permission. This he preferred. "Of course. Can I ask what your reservations are?"

"Truthfully?"

"I think I was very truthful with you just now."

"You're a man who spends his life in the spotlight. You have been since you won your first Formula One race. The spotlight is not something I'm…comfortable with. If I accept your offer—and that is a decidedly big 'if'— you have to understand that all my guidance and direction will be behind the scenes."

"I don't care about what happened with you and him," he offered.

"I don't discuss what happened. Ever. I'm simply giving you my working parameters."

"But you'll stay here. In Detroit. With me."

She seemed to consider that deeply, as if she just realized what her commitment would mean. "Yes. But the only people who would know about my involvement are myself, Ben and anyone you consider essential. I draw these lines not only for my protection but for yours. Your image might not be helped if people knew I was working with you."

"*For* me," he corrected. "You would be working for me. I want to make sure you understand that. I'll do whatever you say that makes sense. But I'm not some puppet blindly taking orders."

She tilted her head slightly to the right as if scrutinizing him. As though she was Dr. Frankenstein and was coldly, clinically wondering if he had any potential as a monster.

"I'll call you first thing in the morning."

"I look forward to it." He stood and stretched out his hand. She accepted it as she stood. Her grasp was firm and strong and brief.

Too brief. He didn't know if it was him, or whether letting go so fast was something she'd trained herself to do. He only knew he missed her touch when it was gone.

"Goodbye, Mr. Langdon."

"See you soon, Ms. Kane."

His choice of words was deliberate and they weren't lost on her. She gave him a brief smile, straightened her suit jacket and walked out his office door.

He was right. He didn't like the feeling of seeing her leave. But he had confidence she would be back. He wasn't wrong in his description of her. She was a kingmaker and he was a man who would be king—at least in this arena.

Sitting, he turned to the flat screen on his office wall and pulled up the specs of his electric car. It moved and rotated, showing him each side. It was a thing of beauty. It was revolutionary. It was going to change the driving experience for the millions of people who would buy it.

But right now it wasn't capturing his attention half so much as the woman who'd just left his office.

MADELEINE OPENED THE door to her hotel room and felt a sense of relief when the door closed behind her. She was staying in one of the best hotels in downtown Detroit, not too far from Michael Langdon's offices. The room was like any other she'd spent her life in so many years ago. Two beds, a desk, an uncomfortable chair, with meaningless, boring art covering the walls.

The sentimental side of her said it was good to be in familiar surroundings again.

It felt good to kick off her shoes and take off her suit jacket. It had been a long time since she'd actually had to meet with a client and needed the barrier of formal business attire. In her opinion, nothing said "back off" like a woman in a buttoned up, dark colored business suit.

Checking her watch she could see it was just after six. Ben would hopefully still be up. She extracted her tablet from her briefcase. Calling his number, she hit the button to interface. If Ben was up, which was likely given the time, he would either be sitting at his desk or would have his tablet with him in bed.

"Why do you insist on calling me like this?"

His voice was gruff, but still as strong as it was when she'd left. She'd caught him in his office.

"I like to see your shiny bald head. It makes me smile."

"I think you're afraid when I die Anna is going to simply record my voice and run the business on her own and you'll never know she's got me buried in the backyard."

"Hardee, har." Anna's voice came from off

the view of the computer's camera. "Death humor. I love it."

It was comforting to know Anna would never leave Ben's side. She was either the most dedicated assistant in all the world, or his very best friend. Sometimes it was hard to tell.

The redhead popped her face over Ben's shoulder. "Hi, Mad. So what do you think? Ready to come out of obscurity and take the world by storm again?"

"Don't pressure her," Ben said, shooing Anna away with his hand.

"I'm going to make your dinner. What do you want?"

"Nothing," he growled, not looking at the computer but at his assistant, who was once again off camera.

"Steak and mashed potatoes? With asparagus in hollandaise sauce? That's exactly what I was thinking."

"Please, God, tell me you're not going to attempt to cook that."

"Uh, duh. It's called delivery."

Madeleine smiled. She shouldn't have been worried about leaving him. Not with Anna there. "I see you are in good hands."

"I'm in impossible hands. I fire her daily, yet she keeps coming back. She knows I don't have the strength to physically remove her and I find that absolutely galling."

Madeleine took note of the flannel robe and the lines around Ben's mouth and eyes. He'd been a superhero once. First a servant to his country, then a man who charged in and rescued people from their failing lives. Now his life was failing and Madeleine wondered what the group would do without him.

Not that everyone in the Tyler Group wouldn't ultimately recover. Everyone Ben hired had a unique skill set that would always be valuable to people who needed that particular service. What Ben provided that no one else could, however, were the connections. Putting people together who needed each other the most. That was his special skill.

She shivered a little and hoped he hadn't seen it. She needed to think positive thoughts. "How is the treatment going?"

"Treatment sucks."

"So I've been told. What are the doctors saying?"

"I don't want to talk about the doctors, I want to talk about you and the job. What did you think of Michael?"

Where to begin? Her impressions raced through Madeleine's mind at lightning speed. Handsome, intelligent, forceful, tightly wound.

Not too dissimilar to the politicians she used to work with back in the day. The differences were subtle but they were there. Michael was not as polished. The Armani suit, which was tailored perfectly for him, still didn't quite fit. His language wasn't always refined, though there was no hint of the streets where, according to his famous bio, he apparently grew up.

The boy from 8 Mile who went from stealing cars to becoming a legend in the racing world to creating an empire of specialty high-end vehicles sought out by millionaires and billionaires around the world.

Now he was ready to turn his talents to mass marketing a car for the future. It was ambitious and noble, probably unlikely. Definitely unlikely considering the world still saw him as a frivolous speed jockey who liked to drink champagne from women's cleavage after each victory.

Strange, but the man who had sat across from her hadn't looked much like the pictures she'd seen when doing preliminary research. His hair was natural brown with gold streaks rather than bleached white, as it had been during his days on the racing circuit. While his hazel eyes had been more prominent with the extreme color, they seemed fairly normal on a face that wasn't as darkly tanned as it had been back then.

Of course, in most pictures he'd always been wearing his custom-made trademark wraparound sunglasses. No real chance for a person to see his eyes and detect the intelligence and determination within them.

"He was okay."

"*Okay.* What an abysmal word. Talk to me, Madeleine."

She wasn't sure what to say. "He's got potential. If he plays his cards right and changes his public persona, I think he would stand a better chance of having his ideas reach his target audience."

"Does he need your help to do that?"

Yes. Madeleine was confident about that. She was sure he didn't see himself the way she did. "I think so. You know my concerns."

"I know your concerns. I also know what it meant for you to leave your house to fly out there and meet him. And I appreciate that you did it because I asked. But, Madeleine, it's been seven years."

She hated when people recited the number. It was like there was some magical timetable in the universe for recovery. After two years she should have moved on. After five years she should have put it in perspective.

After seven years she should have forgotten it entirely.

None of those things had happened. It made her feel weak. She hated feeling weak more than she hated people reciting the number of years since the incident.

"I'm considering it." She would sleep on it and decide if the fear of getting back into this line of work outweighed her need to do more than simply read or write about a subject.

"Good girl. This job would be good for you. I know it. And Michael...well, Michael's not what he seems. You know how the media can distort things."

"You mean like when they christened me the 'Whore of the Twenty-first Century'?"

Ben actually smiled. "Yeah. Like that. When you think about how ridiculous the name— It doesn't matter. You can't go back. Only forward. I've been letting you bury your head in the sand for five years coming up with idea after idea that other people take credit for. That time is over, Madeleine. You're ready."

"Thanks, Pop." It was a lecture she had received before, mainly from herself. She bristled a little to hear it from Ben.

She understood she'd purposefully cut herself off from the life she once had. But it wasn't as if anyone had come knocking on her door to pull her back into the political arena. She could be as ready to reenter the political world as can be. It didn't mean she was going to get any job offers.

"I'm not your father, I'm your employer. More importantly, I know you. Go research electric cars and Michael because you know you are itching to do it. Then call him in the morning and take the job. Consider my health-care costs. I need the money."

Madeleine snorted. Ben Tyler did not need the money. He did, however, need to think he was contributing to the group, helping its members. Especially at a time when he felt so physically useless.

"I'm seriously considering it," she told him.

"I'll take it."

"Yo, cancer boy. Dinner is on the way and you are going to eat some of it even if I have to sit on your pathetically weak chest and force the food down."

Ben leaned into the camera and lowered his voice. "Do you see what I have to put up with?" To Anna he shouted, "You're fired."

"Nice try, Donald Trump. Start making your way into the kitchen. By the time you shuffle here the food will have arrived."

Madeleine laughed and she could see a hint of a smile on Ben's face before she disconnected the call. That was what made Anna completely indispensable. She still made Ben smile. And a man, no matter how sick, still wanted to smile once in a while.

Left on her own, Madeleine thought about Michael. Michael, who needed a kingmaker.

This was probably not going to end well, but the urge to reach for it was impossible to ignore. For seven years she'd felt like she was living someone else's life. Happily, because her own life had imploded into a disaster. Lately, though, she'd begun to feel a sense of urgency. Like if she didn't try to overcome her fears she would waste away and forever become the quiet hermit she'd made herself into.

She was going to take the job.

God help her.

CHAPTER TWO

"THIS IS IT."

Madeleine turned her attention to the flat-screen monitor on the wall and watched a series of images appear. At Michael's urging, she'd agreed to come back to his office for an in-depth look at the project. Despite having made up her mind to take the job, she still found herself hesitating to tell him.

Sitting with him now, the presentation was less important than observing the man. She watched as he animatedly went through each screen, detailing design changes, enhancements and improvements for the standard Detroit-made car, while at the same time utilizing the factory machinery already in place. He talked about making more space in the passenger seating area and trunk without the need for driveshafts and chassis.

None of it made any sense to her. She was the stereotypical woman when it came to automobiles. She knew they needed a key and gas to work and every three thousand miles the oil needed to be changed. That was about all.

"Okay, let's talk about money. Are you still with me?"

Madeleine nodded, then listened to him expand on costs. He discussed how many to build against projections of what would sell. And the price of the car and the impact it would have on the average American. Not to mention the nation's dependence on foreign oil.

Madeleine had to smother a smile. The average American. It had been a long time since she'd heard anyone use that phrase so effectually. Because it targeted not a specific group, but everyone in the country. It was something politicians learned long ago, all American people, rich, poor and those in the middle, still liked to identify themselves as average.

This man wasn't average. He was extraordinary.

Again she considered the bio on him she had read before agreeing to fly to Detroit. Raised by a single mother in the poor section of Detroit, he found he had a knack for both fixing up cars as well as racing them. It eventually led him into crime when he began to steal them. Incarcerated at the age of nineteen, he'd served all three years of his sentence.

His time served was actually an anomaly. As a first-time offender for grand theft auto, the sentence made perfect sense. But with parole and relatively good behavior he should have been out in half the time. Instead he'd spent the full three years behind bars.

After being released he went to work at an auto body shop. Archie Beeker still owned and operated it, not too far from where Michael grew up. In countless interviews, Michael always credited Archie with giving him his start, with saving his life. While working for Archie he began to rebuild cars from the scrap heap and was racing them in what was called "Formula X" races all around the country.

Not the sleek, sophisticated machines of Formula One and not the stock racing cars of NASCAR, the Formula X cars represented the best designs built with the least amount of money. Eventually through his wins and his designs, Michael attracted the attention of a Formula One team who took him to Europe and the rest was history. After years of successfully racing cars in Europe he eventually retired and came back to his hometown of Detroit to start up his specialty car design company. A company that would eventually spawn the idea for the vehicle he was currently showing her.

Madeleine tried to reconcile the images of the spiky-white-haired racer with the wraparound shades and the sedate businessman standing in front of her in his expensive suit and tie.

But there were still edges to the businessman. His sleeves were rolled up. She could see his forearms were sprinkled with light brown hair. For a moment she was captivated by those naked arms.

"So what do you think?"

She thought his arms appeared very strong. Probably not the answer he was looking for and definitely not something she should be thinking about at all. In fact, she couldn't remember the last time she'd had such thoughts about a man. Probably not in seven years.

Another kind of counting she didn't like to think about. She didn't know what the fact that it had been so long said about her, a woman who hadn't admired a man's forearms in more than seven years.

Cold? Most likely. Overly cautious? Definitely.

"Have I finally convinced you?" he asked.

"I think you believe in what you're doing."

"Understatement. Did I sell you?"

"I don't know much about auto mechanics."

"Forget that, did I sell you as an average citizen? Would you buy this car? Would you believe you can save money by buying it?"

Madeleine considered that. She drove a BMW. A nine-year-old gift from her father, which was beginning to show its age. He'd given it to her after she'd been hired by the Marlin presidential campaign. Tangible evidence of her success at such a young age. Her older brother, Robert, who hadn't yet made junior partner at his law firm, had been seething with jealousy when her father handed her the keys.

She should have done away with it years ago, if only because it brought back memories of a time when her father was proud of her. Not that she was hanging on to it for sentimental reasons, trying to hold on to a piece of him now that he was gone.

Her father would disdain such impracticality.

The future was where her head should be. Eco-friendly instead of maudlin and sappy. What Michael was describing would be better than all hybrids on the road today. Definitely a practical choice for her.

"I don't know," she said, trying to regain her focus on the present instead of the past. "It almost seems improbable."

"Exactly! That's my point. We get it into our heads that technology is so far down the road we think it will always be out of reach. I want to convince people the time is here and now. We can have this." He pointed to the screen, now an image of a silver car anybody would want to own. "We can have this now."

"Then let's talk about the other side of the equation. Tell me about you."

"Why do I feel like I'm the one being interviewed?"

"Because you are. Remember, I need to believe in you as well as your project. You've sold me on the project, now sell me on you."

"I'm the problem, remember? It's why I need you. I'm a hard-drinking, fast-car driving, womanizing playboy."

No, she thought, he wasn't. There was so much more to him. She could sense it. There was a sincerity about him that playboys she'd met, and she'd met plenty during her days on political campaigns, never had. "You also run a successful luxury-car company. One wonders where you find the time for all your activities."

"A man finds time for what he wants. And

I no longer actually race fast cars, at least not competitively, so there's that."

"Why do I feel like you want me to see the worst in you?" She could see the question startled him, but she sensed it was getting closer to the truth.

"I don't. I'm trying to be honest here."

"Hmm," she murmured. Again, she didn't think so. Instinctively she felt like he was hiding something. It should have signaled her warning bells. After all, she hadn't verbally committed to the job so it wasn't too late to decline his offer. Instead she found herself desperately curious about him.

"If you won't tell me about the man you are today, tell me about who you were. Many have retold your success story. Kid from the wrong side of 8 Mile Road makes it big. How did that happen? How did you turn it around? You were a kid from a poor neighborhood…"

"I was a poor kid," he interrupted.

"Isn't that what I said?"

"No. There is a big difference. There were kids who grew up in the same neighborhood I did who didn't think they were poor. They had a mom, sometimes a dad, too. They had siblings and family meals. They ate three times a day and they went to school and did their homework. Yeah, maybe they wore shoes long after they outgrew them or pants that were too tight. They never got an extra helping at dinner, but they weren't poor."

"You were different from them."

"In every way. It was just me and my mom. Don't ask me about my father, I have no idea who he is."

"I'm sorry."

"I'm not. He could have made things worse. As for my mother, it feels weird calling her that, mostly I called her Jackie. She was an addict. Big deal, right? So are lots of mothers on that side of town. Jackie was strung out most days doing whatever it took to get her next fix, while I survived on what the state gave us. I lived on Kraft Dinner and the dollar menu at the local fast-food place. We never talked from as far back as I could remember. It was like we didn't even know each other. We were two people sharing the same apartment."

"Did you go to school?"

"I tried for a while. I had this thought that I could use school to get out, but it was too much time spent sitting around talking and not enough doing. So I was done with that by seventeen. The only thing I cared about were cars and driving them fast. It's how I got hooked up with Nick. He lived on the block and would see me screeching around town in my mother's POS. He showed me how to fix cars, and my mother's POS always needed fixing. Eventually he brought me into the game."

"Auto theft?"

"Yeah, yeah. At first I just broke down the cars for parts. Then one day Nick takes me out and shows me how to jack them. I'm not going to lie—it was a pretty big high. My adrenaline would pump, but you had to make your fingers move and you had to remember how each car was different and how to shut down an alarm in seconds. In hindsight it was a blessing and a curse."

"A blessing?"

"Kept me off the drugs. Nick didn't tolerate that. Bad for business. No drinking, no drugs. When you jacked you needed full control of your senses."

"The *hard* drinking came later, then?"

"Huh? Oh…yeah, yeah. Later."

Exactly. He was no more a hard-drinking man than she was a hard-drinking woman. Yes, he was definitely hiding something and it was only one of the reasons she was cautious about taking him on as a project.

For one, he was a man in the media spotlight, which meant working with him was going to present some risk. Plus, while she didn't exactly believe he was the scoundrel he presented himself to be, there were all those pictures of him at various parties with so many different women. Men, she found, didn't easily give up the things they wanted—especially when they were told by someone else not to indulge.

But what she had to concern herself with most of all was that she liked the way he looked in his suit. She liked it even better when he rolled up his sleeves. As an employee she should have no physical attraction to her employer. Certainly no emotional attachment.

If it was too late to prevent the physical attraction, she should back out now. It was the only sensible decision.

"What do you say?"

"I'll do it."

The words were out before she could stop them. She couldn't help herself. She felt caught up in his infectiousness. She wanted to stand up and give everyone a new car. More than that she wanted to show everyone what a person who was committed to something could accomplish, no matter what the odds.

An inner voice told her she'd tried that before. *Look at where it led you.*

But that was seven years ago. Maybe it was time she started counting, after all.

"That's great. That's very cool. I'm… pleased."

Madeleine nodded. She reached into her briefcase and pulled out a contract. "This is a standard contract from the Tyler Group. It breaks down my rates, services and expenses. You should have your attorneys look it over."

"Yeah, yeah." He signed and dismissed the paper without even looking at it.

"I hate to be blunt, but you really should consider going over the contract first. The Tyler Group isn't cheap and my rider, while not diva level, is still extensive."

"I don't want cheap. I want the best. I'll pay whatever you're asking. It's done."

Madeleine smiled. "That will make Ben happy. Okay, then we should establish a time to start."

"Right now."

"Now? Surely you have other matters to attend to and will need to rearrange your calendar, Mr. Langdon."

"It's Michael. And I don't. This is the most important thing to me. I know this is going to take time. You don't change your image over-night. The sooner we get started, the sooner I get what I want. The CEOs I'm trying to convince aren't easy pushovers. I'm talking about Carter, Blakely, Rodgers and Smith-field."

The current leaders of the four largest car companies in America. He was right, con-vincing one of those men to take a risk would be hard enough, convincing one of them to take a risk with him was something alto-gether difficult. Maybe impossible. But he had her on his side.

Madeleine pulled out her laptop and pow-ered it up. "Well, we need to begin with my parameters. As I said, I don't intend to have anything to do with your spotlight. I will not do PR from the front line. I will not do direct media interviews or issue press releases in my name. I will, however, work my media contacts and connect you with the people I think can help, but I will do so discreetly."

"Yeah, yeah. But hear me out. I know the whole big scandal and everything."

That was one way to describe it.

"Before all that, you were really respected. Revered even. I'm thinking you hanging around a bum like me might be a good thing. Your presence alone could gain me respect."

She could see in his eyes that he truly believed what he was saying. A flush of emotion overcame her and for a moment she feared she would tear up. She swallowed it and took a breath.

"While I appreciate the sentiment, Mr. Langdon…"

"Michael. Please say my name."

His tone took her off guard. Not annoyed. Not angry. Merely insistent.

"Michael." The name came out of her mouth sounding like a sigh. "I don't think you understand the magnitude of what happened. Trust me when I tell you being seen with the former president's mistress will not gain you any public-relations points. If anything it will make you more of a joke."

"So you slept with your boss. It's not the first time that's ever happened. It's not like you're Jezebel."

According to her father she was. In fact it was the last word he'd ever said to her.

"It doesn't matter. You need to trust me. My presence will not help you. My advice can. You wanted to know where to start?"

"Yes."

"Then we start with the people who gave you your image in the first place. You'll need to use the media—only this time on your terms. You'll need to identify several well-known charities you can link your name with."

"I already have a charity."

Madeleine knew he donated generously to a jobs program that helped inmates transition when they left prison. "Yes, but we'll need something more high profile. I know it sounds self-serving and the idea of charity is to be selfless, but in this case we have no choice. I'm thinking environmental causes. Attaching yourself to the green movement will seem to give you purpose when you present your idea to the people you want to partner with. It raises the stakes on the whole project."

Michael stood and paced a little behind his desk while Madeleine used her computer to call up events that might be newsworthy.

"There, in two days. And bonus—it's local. There is a charity being hosted by Solarcomp. They are the group that promotes…"

"I know who they are."

"For five thousand dollars a plate you can attend, for twenty thousand a plate you can sit at a table with the former vice president who believes solar energy is the key to our clean-energy future."

Michael stopped his pacing and faced

her. "I'm not opposed to the environmental causes."

"That's good. Few people are."

"I meant… I want you to know…*you*…that I'm not launching this car for purely altruistic reasons. I'm a businessman. I have what I believe is a good idea. I want to make money from it. If in the end it saves people money and helps the environment that's gravy, but it's not what I'm about."

Madeleine looked at him. "Why do you think it's important I should know that?"

"I don't want to be a fraud to you. I don't want you to think I'm something I'm not."

Madeleine considered that. "I think you're a businessman, in need of a new reputation. I think your cause is worthy and I've already accepted the position. You don't have to prove anything to me, Mr.…"

"Don't do it."

"Michael. You don't have anything to prove to me, Michael."

"Of course I don't. I wanted you to know the score. That's all."

"Okay. Well, let's talk about Solarcomp's Night of Lights event. According to the website I can still get you two seats at the five-thousand-dollar level. Given the attendees it should definitely garner some media attention. Plus, the former vice president has a new book coming out. We need to talk about your escort."

"Escort? That's an old-fashioned word."

"Your date."

"That can't be you? Right?"

Madeleine felt a zing of reaction whiz through her body. She wasn't sure if it was fear, revulsion at the idea of being seen at an event or something else she wasn't going to put a name to.

She met his eyes and searched them for meaning. When he looked back at her directly she could see his intentions. He wasn't asking her on a date. He was simply reiterating his point that he thought it was a good idea to be seen with her.

He was wrong.

"Michael, do you trust me to do my job?"

"Of course. You wouldn't be here otherwise."

"Then please don't ever ask me something like that again. I've told you I'm poison. I mean this not in a self-deprecating way, but in the cold, hard fact way."

"Maybe I want a beautiful woman on my arm."

"Do an internet search on your name, then click the images page. I'm sure you'll find you always have a beautiful woman on your arm."

He dug his hands into his pants pockets and said nothing.

"We need to talk about who she will be."

"I don't know," he said, shaking his head. "I'm not really involved with anyone right now."

"Do you have any ideas of who you might call? Anyone who could be available on short notice?"

He met her eyes steadily. "There are a few who would come on short notice. Why does it matter?"

"Because one of the things we want to try to countermand is your playboy image. A different girl every week, every event, every red carpet, lends itself to that. If you could possibly settle on one…"

Michael's jaw dropped. "You want me to start a relationship with a woman because it would be good for my reputation?"

Madeleine inwardly sighed. She was working with an amateur. Which meant she needed patience. Amateurs didn't understand that everything counted. Every word, every action, every picture printed in the media, was its own story. To create an image one had to be in control of every element of his life. What he said, what he ate, who he saw publicly. Politicians knew this. To a certain extent so did the Hollywood elite, although their cultivated image was often more radical than a politician's.

She had to admit she was a little stunned by how quickly and easily it all came back. After years of researching and writing position papers, here she was, doing what she knew how to do best. It was thrilling and daunting considering who she had to work with. But to have a challenge, a real challenge in her life, she could feel the adrenaline pulsing beneath her skin.

"Of course not. I want you to consider if there is a woman in your life who you are more partial to than others. Being seen with the same woman at multiple events implies a relationship even if there truly isn't one. It shows stability, maturity and lends itself to the new image we want to cultivate for you, that you are someone to be trusted."

"Wow. That's pretty…cold."

Madeleine stood and closed her laptop. "Michael, everything you do from now on will be screened by me. I'll determine your tie-color choice, the events where you will be seen and yes, if I can have some say in the woman you choose to escort to these events, that will be helpful. There is no emotion in these decisions, no personal stake. I'm going to help you tell the best story you can and the rest is up to you. Are you still certain you want to do this?"

"I have no choice, do I?"

Madeleine shook her head. "We always have choices."

"Is that what you told yourself when it all came crashing down around you? That your choices led to your fall?"

She didn't detect any bitterness in his question. Merely curiosity. So she answered him.

"It's exactly what I told myself."

MICHAEL WATCHED HER leave with the same twitchy feeling he suffered the day before. Only this time it was easy to shake it off since he knew she would be back. What was it about her?

She was right: he was used to attractive women. Women more glamorous, more blatantly sexual. On the two days he'd seen her, she had been wearing a dark gray business suit then a black business suit. Both austere, both unassuming. She could have been an FBI agent for all her flash. Still when she was around him, he felt something.

Something instinctual.

Free to pace now that she was gone, he

trod back and forth in his plushly carpeted office. He never liked to overdo it in front of people. He only ever allowed himself a few back-and-forths before forcing himself to stay still. Pacing could be construed as a sign of nerves or anxiety, which obviously wasn't something he wanted to communicate to people. For him it was a bad habit. One he picked up in prison as a way to deal with being confined in a cell. As long as he kept moving he could cope with the tight space. It was when he stopped that he felt like the walls would start to close in on him.

So Madeleine wanted him to take a woman to the charity event. And not just any woman. But a woman he might consider taking to more than a handful of events. A woman he might consider spending enough time with that the media could start using the word *relationship*.

The idea was laughable. The women were there for a purpose. He knew she thought he was naive at the game they were playing, creating an image, manipulating the press to think what he wanted them to think, but the truth was he was a master craftsman.

At least at creating the bad-boy persona. He knew how to present himself so people would see what he wanted them to see. He didn't know how to do that and come off as respectable. That's why he'd reached out to Ben.

Michael knew Madeleine Kane was a member of Ben's team and he knew about the scandal involving her and the president peripherally. He'd been in Europe at the time and his racing career had started its meteoric rise. An American sex scandal made the news, but in Europe they always thought Americans took sex too seriously so the story was only casually mentioned.

If a man had a mistress, so be it. If the woman chose to be that mistress, her choice. The president was a powerful man. Who wouldn't want his attention?

Michael tried to reconcile the woman in his office with the star of the scandal. She was so buttoned up. So locked down as if every word she said and every movement she made was carefully considered. How had a woman like that tempted the president?

What the hell was he saying? She only had to look at Michael and he was... He didn't know what he was. He couldn't say aroused. Maybe intrigued. Something.

He needed information. Sitting at his desk he called up a search engine and started to type. It wasn't difficult. Key in *Madeleine*

Kane and *President* and there were hundreds of pictures, articles and blogs related to the subject.

She wasn't overplaying the size of the scandal. Looking at the time frame, it had gone on for months. Even after she'd resigned and the First Lady filed for divorce from President Marlin, the press continued to pursue her. Unlike his predecessor, who had once been in the center of a sexual scandal, this president didn't lie about the affair. He came clean quickly and apologized profusely.

No crime had been committed and as a result no charges of impeachment were filed against him. After several months it died a slow death and he went about the job of running the country. He was not reelected but Michael thought that had more to do with his jobs policy than it did the sex scandal.

Madeleine never reentered the political arena and after a two-year hiatus in media attention, there was a blip of an article announcing her addition to the Tyler Group.

Not a surprise Ben would go after her. He collected great minds like most people collected coins. His group was part think tank, part troubleshooters, all brains. If someone needed a job done and didn't have the skills or the necessary people on hand to accomplish the task, they contacted Ben.

The Tyler Group was like a brainy version of the A-Team. Selling their specific set of skills for a price.

In Europe, Michael had met Ben while he was still an operative for the CIA. Michael actually liked to think he'd helped him out on a mission, but all he'd really done was act as a carrier pigeon. Still, it was as close to James Bond as he'd ever gotten. For whatever reason, Ben had seen through the image of the hard-drinking, hard-gambling, hard-sexing playboy. As though he'd been wearing special-colored glasses.

At first he had balked at Ben's request that Michael help him out. Until the idea of doing something right for a good cause settled in his stomach and made him feel…better about himself.

Ben thought he was in Michael's debt. The reality was the opposite. Meeting Ben and getting to know him helped Michael grow up. Ben wasn't just some government agent. He was a man who cared deeply about his country and the work he did for it. It had been such a simple chore he'd asked Michael to do. When Michael asked, "Why me?" Ben said it was time for Michael to do something for someone else.

He'd been right. And it had been another step in the path that had eventually helped him to get his life back when it seemed as if prison had taken it all away.

At least part of his life.

Michael finally pushed away from the computer, tired of reading the sordid details of Madeleine's past. Somehow he doubted the affair was quite as dirty as the press made it out to be. One article mentioned toys, another the president's need to be dominated, of all things.

He could see Madeleine wielding a whip. He couldn't imagine her doing something as silly as smacking a man's bare ass with it.

No, if Madeleine was going to take out a whip she would have a much more useful purpose. Michael smiled as he shut down his computer. After a moment he got up and started pacing again.

Right, then left. Right, then left.

CHAPTER THREE

"How are things going with the new girl?"

Michael handed down a crescent wrench to Archie. Instantly an image of Madeleine appeared in his mind, but Archie didn't know anything about Madeleine. No one did.

She was like the Wizard of Oz behind the curtain secretly pulling all the strings. Any consulting was done either by phone or occasionally after hours in his office. Mostly she coached him on answers to questions that might be put to him when a microphone was shoved in his face. And of course she was always plotting ways to get him to those places where the microphones might be.

He'd asked her to visit his home in Grosse Pointe. He thought she could stay in one of his guest rooms, which would be more comfortable than a sterile hotel suite. She'd stiffened and told him in no uncertain terms that there was not a single reason for her to see his personal residence.

No stepping out of bounds for his girl.

Not his girl.

She wasn't even remotely his girl. Still, he couldn't stop thinking about her. A condition that was becoming as problematic as it was annoying.

"Which new girl?"

"The one you went to that fancy shindig with. The actress. What's her name. You know, she was in that movie with that fancy guy."

"Charlene Merritt. She was in a movie with George Clooney."

"Yeah, that guy. He's sharp. No Cary Grant, but then who is today?"

"Really, Archie? You're that old you remember Cary Grant?"

The dolly slid out from under the car. A small, thin white-haired old man with bifocals squinted up at him. "*North by Northwest, Charade, Psycho*...now those were real movies."

"I'm pretty sure Cary Grant wasn't in *Psycho.*"

Archie waved him off. "Oh, what do you know."

Michael pulled out his smartphone to check, but then tucked it away. No reason to upstage the man.

"So you like this girl or what?"

"Charlene is very beautiful."

"You've been with her to two things now. You never see a girl two times in a row. I think you like this one."

Michael had flown Charlene in for the Solarcomp charity event. Then he'd taken her to dinner at The Whitney where they had been photographed together. Madeleine had been pleased.

"I like her all right."

"But do you *like* her like her? You're not getting any younger, kid. It's time you start thinking about settling down and getting yourself some kids."

The concept was so far removed from Michael's reality there was no point in even refuting it. Instead he said, "My focus is on getting this electric car off the ground. Not getting married. Charlene is hanging around. She likes to be wined and dined. There is nothing serious there."

Archie offered his hand and Michael pulled on it until the man was sitting and then on his feet. Archie took a rag out of his pocket, wiped his hands more out of habit than need and shuffled his feet a few times.

"I've known you a long time, Mickey."

Twenty years. They'd met back when he'd been Mickey Lang because someone along the way thought the name Langdon was too fancy for 8 Mile.

"You're not about to lecture me, are you, Archie?"

"I'm saying you've come through a lot. And now you're on top of the world. You're like that guy…what's that fellow…the one on the boat. You can hold your arms up and say you're the king. But still I look at you and I don't see a happy guy. I think maybe a wife, kids…a family. This would make you happy."

"You're my family, Archie."

"Ah, kid, don't get all sentimental on me. I'm not dying yet. I'll let you know when I am and then you can come cry over my bed and say nice things to me. I'm saying a man reaches an age when the money isn't enough."

"What happened to you, then? What woman wouldn't have wanted all this?" Michael looked around the run-down mechanic's shop. Through rose-colored glasses Archie saw it as a thriving business when in fact it was a dump. Michael had offered Archie all the money in the world to take on more help, to fix the place up nice.

The old man would have none of it. After all, if he actually brought on full-time help, where would the ex-cons go to find honest work when they got out?

"I'm an ex-con, Mickey. I didn't have much of a choice. You come clean with a lady about that and she's likely to run the other way."

"I'm an ex-con," Michael reminded him.

"Yeah, but you washed all the stink right off. Hell, they talk about you being in prison like you were out on a picnic. You're like a reformed version of…who was that guy in the movies, the one with the funny voice. James Cagney, yeah, like him. Bad boy makes good. I read the magazines. I know."

"Prison wasn't a picnic," Michael said thickly as a surge of shame and disgust rose up in his throat. *This,* he thought, *this is why I will never have a family. I can never leave it behind.*

The irritating part was that he'd accepted that fact years ago, but now when he thought about Madeleine things started resurfacing. Wishes and desires he thought he'd squashed forever. With them came regret and loss. It was why in some ways being around her was pure hell.

"Well, you do what you want. Are you going to see what's-her-face again?"

"Charlene?"

"Yeah, that one."

"One more time. She's accompanying me to the Detroit Revival event."

Archie laughed. "If I had a nickel every time they said Detroit was making a comeback I wouldn't need to play the lottery every day, that's for sure."

"Maybe this time they're right. A new type of car, manufacturing on the rise. Hell, even the Lions are winning. Who knows what's possible?"

Archie shook his head.

Michael reached into his back pocket. "Speaking of the lottery. I almost forgot. These are for you."

"Kid, why do you keep doing this?"

"They're scratch offs. I buy them for me and I get tired of scratching."

Archie took the five cardboard pieces. "You got a dime? Or a quarter? A nickel won't work on these."

Michael jangled some of the loose change in his pocket. He pulled out a quarter and watched as the man leaned against the old Chevy to carefully scratch each square.

One of these days he would hit. Michael was sure of it.

"Hey, look at this! Two bucks. I'm on a roll."

The rest of them proved worthless, but

now Archie had cash for two more. He was a happy man.

"Listen, I have to go out of town for a while as soon as the Revival thing is over. When I'm back I'll stop by."

"Yeah. Okay. I've got a new project coming in a couple of days and it would be nice if you could meet him."

By "new project," Archie meant a guy out on probation. Archie liked to think that Michael could rub off on an ex-con and maybe make a difference. Hell, maybe he did, Michael didn't really know. Most of Archie's projects came for a couple of months and then left. Either to find a better job that actually paid something or to return to the life they knew before. Michael rarely followed up with any of them.

It was easy to give money to a charity that offered support for people getting out of jail, but it was never easy spending time with actual ex-cons. It reminded him too much of his past.

"Sure. I'll come over when he gets here. But I'll check in on you, too, when I get back."

"Whatever. It's not like I need to be watched over by you, kid. I do the watching. You hear me."

"Yeah, yeah. I'm saying when I get back

maybe we can head over to Darnell's for some barbecue. We haven't done that in a while."

"Darnell's? It's a date."

"A date, huh? I don't know. You're no-where near as pretty as Charlene."

"Get out of here, kid. Before I show you all the ways I know how to use a crescent wrench."

Michael lifted his hands in surrender and left the shop. He got into his specially for-mulated Chrysler, one he'd rebuilt from the ground up, and tossed the kid who had watched it for him a couple of bucks.

Beeker's wasn't in the greatest part of town, but it wasn't in the worst, either. Archie lived right on the edge. And for the most part, people around these parts looked at Michael as a local hero. The money for the kid had been more about finding a way to hand out a few bucks than keeping his rims safe.

Once Michael closed the door behind him, he hit the car's start button and did one last check to make sure Archie was where he al-ways was. The man joked about not dying, but he was over seventy and he wouldn't be around forever.

Once Michael had tried to talk him into a place in Florida but that idea went over as well as offering him money to fix up the shop. Archie Beeker wanted to die while changing somebody's oil. It was the way it was. Michael had to hope his death was a long way off. He wasn't kidding when he called Archie family. He sure as hell knew Archie was the only family he would ever have.

"ARE YOU ready for this evening?" Madeleine asked as she hit the speaker button on her phone and set it down on the coffee table in her hotel room. In an act of small defiance, she shucked off her shoes before sitting on the couch.

As a matter of professionalism, she preferred to be in business dress at all times when dealing with a client, even when she was on the phone. The rule was for her sake entirely. It helped keep her mind focused on the job at hand.

But after a long day of airports and cabs, she was happy to be off her feet. Losing the pumps wouldn't completely compromise her professional integrity. She was fairly sure. Besides, it's not like he could see her.

"I have a tux on. I suppose that makes me ready."

Madeleine recalled the pictures of Michael

in the paper from the last event. The black
tuxedo had fit him flawlessly. It should have
made him look elegant and sophisticated. Instead it made him look powerful and edgy.
Like someone had harnessed all this raw energy and shoved it into a suit. The camera
loved him.

And his date. The camera loved both of
them.

"You're picking up Charlene at her hotel."

"Yeah, yeah. She's staying at the same
place you are. You want to come down for a
drink before the event?"

It was offered so casually. A drink before
the event. A glass of wine at the bar where
she could meet Charlene Merritt and ask her
if George Clooney was as handsome in person as he was on film. She could go over the
event schedule again with Michael. She could
update him on her trip back to Philadelphia
to see Ben.

She could see Michael and talk with him.

"No, thank you."

"It's just a drink, Madeleine."

She hated the way he said her name. He
added this extra oomph to the last syllable,
dragging it out so that it sounded like Mad-e-
lane. She thought to correct him, but didn't
see the point since he would keep on saying

it his way no matter what. She wasn't sure at what point she'd even given him permission to use her first name. He probably imagined it was acceptable since she could call him Michael.

In fact, he was the only client she'd been on a first-name basis with in five years. Any contact she had with the representatives from the political action committees or lobbying firms had always been brief and very formal. Michael had already gone beyond that.

"You'll be with Charlene. There could be photographers."

"So?"

For a very intelligent man there were times she knew he played thick deliberately. "Michael." It was all she needed to say.

"Right. I know. No cameras. I thought we could catch up. You've been gone for two days."

"Anything happening I should be aware of?"

"No. Just this event tonight. Then we're scheduled to leave for Los Angeles, right?"

"Yes. I picked up some more clothes from my place on my trip back. I'm all set."

They were going to L.A. so Michael could attend a larger charity event hosted by a famous film director. The party was private but there would be paparazzi littering the entrance. Michael was sure to be photographed again. The media would begin to put the pieces of her puzzle together as environmental event after environmental event featured Michael Langdon.

It was convenient he was interested in Charlene. As a star on the rise she was also attracting a lot of attention. The two of them together at the L.A. party would officially launch speculation about a relationship.

From a public-relations point of view, she was thrilled. More than thrilled. Charlene was not only stunning, but also considered one of Hollywood's good girls. Michael looked good next to her, and more importantly, people thought better of him because he was with her.

"You'll be taking Charlene again? To Drearson's party."

"Maybe. I don't know."

Madeleine was about to say something, then stopped. His relationship with the woman was none of her business. She only needed to focus on the image and she sensed forcing the woman on him was the surest way for him to call it off. There was nothing he'd said directly to her, but she had the sense that his interest in Charlene was superficial at best.

Subtly, on the plane ride out to L.A., she would convince him another photo opportunity with the actress would be ideal. What man wouldn't want to be seen in Charlene's company? There had once been rumors that linked her with Clooney but apparently she had turned him down. It seemed to Madeleine any man would be prancing like a peacock with Charlene at his side.

Only Madeleine hadn't once seen Michael prance. And when the pictures were released of them from the Solarcomp event, Charlene had been holding on to his arm and looking up at his face, but Michael had looked…disinterested.

She shook her head. It was a random picture. Anything could have been happening in that moment to distract him.

Madeleine needed to be more focused on what came next. Michael needed to start talking about his ideas, and she needed someone there to write them down. It was her reason for accompanying him to L.A. She still had some media contacts out there, and a host of people it wouldn't hurt her to reconnect with. If she could work some of her old connections in L.A. and New York, she might be able to get him featured on a prime-time news show.

"Was there anything else?" she asked.

"No. I guess I can't think of anything. You sure you're going to be fine? In your room all night? I mean, do you ever leave it? Ever?"

"Of course I do. However, I also don't mind staying in. It's why I demand a suite when I do this work. It gives me more than enough room to stretch out."

She was stretched out on the couch now, with her shoeless feet resting on a pillow. While on the phone with a client.

Shameless hussy, she thought.

"I'm not sure. I think you spend a lot of time by yourself. I thought maybe when we get back I could show you some of Detroit. The good and the bad. Might give you a better sense of who I am."

Spending time with Michael. Getting to know Michael more.

Both very dangerous things. Madeleine wasn't an idiot. Michael was intelligent, passionate, interesting and completely charismatic. There was a reason women all over the world flocked to him. Spending time in his sphere on a social level was bound to lead to her liking him.

Heck, she already did like him. She liked

his energy and his direction. She liked the way he thought about how she might be lonely sitting in her hotel room.

He was a good man. She sensed it about him. Spending more time with him? It would do nothing but lead to trouble.

"We'll see when we get back." It was an easy out and would generate the least amount of resistance. She wasn't sure what Michael's intent was with all these invitations. Were they purely harmless or something more? Either way she needed to keep him at arm's length if only for a little while. This job wouldn't last too much longer. As long as she kept dancing out of his reach, she should be able to accomplish his goal and move on unscathed.

"Okay. How about you check me out? See if this monkey suit looks okay."

Madeleine accepted the FaceTime request on her phone and a blip later she could see Michael standing in what appeared to be a very large closet holding his phone out so she could get the full effect.

It was as she thought. He looked utterly handsome, if a little restrained. She bet the first thing he would do when he got home from this evening would be to remove the jacket and tie and unbutton his cuffs and roll up his sleeves and relax.

Unless, of course, Charlene was with him. She hadn't considered that possibility. She didn't know why. The woman was obviously interested in him to have come all this way. Of course it made sense he would bring her home at the end of the evening. He had probably already done so on their two previous dates.

That thought made her irritated, but she wasn't willing to admit why.

"You look very nice."

"Nice? That's the best you can do? I spent a couple of grand on this suit."

"How about dashing?"

He smirked and she had to be careful not to roll her eyes since she knew he could see her, too.

See her, too! She was still lying on the couch with her shoes off. Instantly she sat up and while she held the phone steady on her face, she moved her feet around until she found one pump and slipped her foot into it.

"What are you doing?"

"Nothing. Just sitting here being forced to feed you compliments."

Where the hell was her other shoe? Her

foot stretched around while she worked to keep her hand steady.

"You've got a weird look on your face."

"After I called you dashing...you've got some nerve. Wait one second." Madeleine shoved the phone against the sofa cushion and then finally found her other shoe. Fully clothed she felt more in control of herself.

An acknowledged nutcase, but in control.

"There. I'm back."

"Hoookay. Well, you have a good night."

"I will."

"Watch a movie or something."

"Your dime."

"I can afford it. Hell, I can afford two movies if you want. I'll call you first thing tomorrow. We can have breakfast before we leave for the airport."

"Or we can meet there. I can certainly get a cab...if you're...if you're otherwise engaged."

She could see his forehead scrunch like he didn't understand what she was saying.

"With Charlene," she clarified.

"Oh. Yeah, yeah. Well, I'll let you know. 'Bye."

The screen went blank before she could reply. And later that night, instead of enjoying the on-demand movie, she spent the whole time wondering what she had seen in his expression right before he closed the connection.

She was almost certain it was sadness.

CHAPTER FOUR

"COME ON! Don't be like that. I came all this way to be with you and you haven't so much as kissed me on the cheek."

Madeleine was on her way back to her hotel suite with a bucket of ice when the sound of a couple engaged in what appeared to be an intimate conversation stopped her. Not wanting to intrude on what was obviously a private moment, she remained still.

"Then I'll kiss you on the cheek and say good-night. Some other time for us maybe."

That voice! She knew that voice. Holy shoot. Peeking around the corner of the hall she saw Michael leaning in to Charlene as if to kiss her.

Immediately she pulled back. What in the hell were they doing outside of her suite? Or more accurately, the suite door next to hers.

Of course. Michael said Charlene was staying in the same hotel. Naturally she'd have a suite, as well. What were the odds she'd be right next door? Apparently very good ones.

The idea that she might actually have to go back to her room, knowing what Charlene and Michael were doing in the room next to hers, was unthinkable.

Although, that she considered it unthinkable was probably not a good thing, either.

Darn it! Madeleine began to consider her lifetime legacy of bad luck, when she heard a noise that was part moan and part sigh.

Female sigh.

"Michael, stop this silliness. Come inside with me."

"I promised I would walk you to your room and I have."

"Yes, and now that I have you here, I want a little more. I always want a little more when I'm with you. You tease me like no other man has ever teased me."

"I don't mean to be a tease, but I can't stay."

"You can if you want to," the actress said in more of a song than a sentence. Madeleine grimaced. She was standing in the hall in a pair of yoga pants and an old T-shirt with fuzzy socks on her feet and her hair in a ponytail. All she had wanted was a little ice to add to what was left of her mineral water and now she was stuck in what might be the most humiliating situation of her life.

Correction. Not the most humiliating situation. Getting caught in the Oval Office with her skirt hiked up around her hips by the First Lady while her husband shouted "oh, baby" at the top of his lungs—that was the *most* humiliating experience. This would be a very distant second.

"Do you know how many men would kill to be in your position right now?"

"I imagine a great many. You're a very beautiful woman, Charlene. This has nothing to do with you. It's poor scheduling."

"You could always sleep on the plane."

Madeleine had to admire the woman's tenacity. The tone of her voice oozed sex. If she were a man she'd certainly be tempted by now.

"Maybe I can convince you with a little… touch."

"Charlene, please."

"Huh. Well, that's never happened to me before."

Resisting the urge to peek around the corner, Madeleine held still, careful not to move the bucket and rattle the melting ice.

"You really don't want me. I mean, wow. I figured you were playing hard to get, but you're not…hard… anything."

Madeleine had a strong suspicion where

Charlene's touch had landed. Awfully bold considering they were in a hallway where anyone could come by with a bucket of ice in her hands.

"Charlene, it's been a long day. I have a longer day tomorrow. I don't mean to be rude, but no, I'm simply not interested in what you're offering."

"That's a first."

"No man has ever told you no?"

A harsh laugh echoed around the corridor. "I've never had to ask to be told no. I think it's what made you so intriguing. You were the first man I ever dated who didn't immediately try to get me into bed. Now I get it. You're not into me. The question remains, why ask me out?"

"I told you. I'm tired…"

"Don't give me tired. I can make a tired man sit back on his haunches and beg like a puppy if I want. You're not gay, are you?"

Madeleine had to choke back the abrupt "no" that wanted to shoot out of her mouth. Michael Langdon, for whatever reason, was not interested in Charlene Merritt but he was decidedly not gay. There was a way he watched her when they worked together. A way his eyes followed her movements, from picking up a pen she'd dropped to crossing her legs.

No gay man would be as fascinated by the female body. Madeleine sensed it in her gut.

"I'm not gay, Charlene. I am through with this conversation, though. I've enjoyed our time together and I appreciate you coming out here on such short notice. Some other time."

"Okay. Sorry. I had to ask. Some other time."

"I'll call you."

"Right."

Charlene's skepticism wasn't misplaced. Madeleine didn't think he had any intention of calling her, either. She heard a key card slide into the door and a second later she heard the door close.

It would take him maybe two or three more seconds to turn and head back to the elevators around the corner and out of sight. She gave him an extra second beyond that, and then Madeleine turned the corner only to find him still standing outside Charlene's door.

Her faint gasp gave her away. He looked up and instantly frowned.

"How long have you been standing there?"

"I, uh, I went to get some ice. What are you doing here?"

Michael walked to her and she didn't have the sense to run. He glanced down into her bucket and saw the glimmering sheen of ice beginning to melt.

"You heard everything."

"I…" Madeleine's shoulders dropped. There really was no point in lying. "I was coming back and heard you two. I didn't realize she was in the suite next to mine. I didn't want to…interrupt."

"I didn't realize she was in the suite next to yours, either. Is that your room…1022?"

"Yes."

"Does it have a minibar?"

"Yes."

"Good thing you brought ice. Where is your key?"

Madeleine handed it over without thinking. Michael took the key and efficiently swiped it through the holder. The green light appeared and he opened the door. Madeleine had no choice but to follow.

He didn't speak or offer any excuses for barging into her hotel room. Instead he tossed the tuxedo jacket he'd been holding over his shoulder onto the couch and crouched down in front of the minibar.

He pulled out two bottles of Jack Daniel's. "Want anything?"

"No."

"Don't drink?"

"Don't drink with clients." Another of the many rules she'd constructed after her fall. Always be professional. Always maintain a certain level of distance. No drinking or socializing. No casual dress.

Madeleine looked down at her fuzzy socks. So much for rules tonight.

"I'll have mineral water."

"Come on, Madeleine, don't make me drink alone. I promise I'll never tell." He pulled out a mini Chardonnay and handed it to her.

For a moment she hesitated. And part of her knew what the problem was. She wanted to take the damn wine. She wanted to sit with him and recap how the event went. She wanted to know what happened with Charlene and why he didn't seem interested.

She wanted to be with him for a time.

For that reason alone she should refuse the wine and politely ask him to leave. But doing so might make her seem a little ridiculous in this situation. He was in her hotel room, she was wearing socks. One glass of wine wasn't going to kill her. Surely a woman in full control of herself could break her own rules occasionally without there being consequences.

She hoped so.

"Okay." She turned over two clean glasses and handed him one. He added ice to his drink and then sat on the couch. She chose the chair across from him.

"Want to tell me what you're doing here?" Madeleine asked.

"Having a drink."

"I thought you were tired and worried about your early flight."

"Since our flight doesn't leave until noon you know that's a bald-faced lie."

Madeleine fidgeted a little as she sipped her wine. Unthinkingly she brought up her legs and tucked them under her butt. When she looked back to Michael she could see even that simple movement fascinated him.

His eyes were also trying very hard not to look at her chest. She had a tank top on but she was most definitely braless.

"Look, I'm sorry if I pushed you toward her. I thought you liked her."

"I did like her. I just didn't want to have sex with her."

"Why?" The question popped out before she could stop it. It was far too personal. His eyebrows arched up as if to suggest he agreed. But for some reason she wanted an answer. "You heard her. She can make a tired man beg like a puppy."

"Maybe I have more discerning tastes." He drank his whiskey in one gulp then opened the second bottle and splashed it over the ice.

"A playboy with discerning tastes. Those two things usually don't go together." Like a lot of things about him, the pieces didn't fit. Madeleine knew all about constructing an image and it was becoming evident that Michael's playboy image was as real as his environmental-philanthropist cover.

"What do you want? What answer are you looking for here? She didn't do it for me. She didn't make my dick hard. I can't make it any plainer than that."

Madeleine winced. Not so much at his harsh language but at the anger she heard in his tone. She didn't know who he was directing his anger toward and she really didn't care. The last thing she wanted to be talking about was sex. Especially with him.

"I didn't mean anything. Truly. We shouldn't be having this conversation, anyway. It's way too personal."

"Eff that. What is it with you and the whole no crossing lines? We're people. We're talking. It's personal. With you everything has a rule."

She snorted. "You really have to ask why?"

"I get it, but it's like you're obsessed. Are you worried that if you let loose a little we're going to pounce on each other? If I see you with your hair down or call you by your name, suddenly I'm going to want to get between your legs?"

"Stop it. That's enough."

He abruptly shut his mouth. He stood and carefully set the now-empty glass down on the table between them.

"I'm sorry."

Madeleine stood, assuming she was going to show him to the door. She should have accepted his apology and said good-night. Instead she felt like she owed him an apology, too. "I know I have boundaries and rules. I put all of them there for a reason."

"But don't you let anyone in? Ever?"

No, she hadn't. She had coworkers she considered friends. There was Ben and Anna, but no, there was really no one she'd let get past her guard in these past seven years. If he knew to what extent, he might think her a freak. But that was her business.

"You have to understand, even before my *fall* I wasn't the greatest at relationships."

"Why not? You're smart and hot to boot. It should have all come so easy for you."

Easy. It was almost laughable. Nothing that wasn't work related had ever come easy for her. Not relationships, not sex. Not ever.

Madeleine shook off her thoughts. That was a place she didn't want to go. Memories that were better left untouched. But he was still standing there looking at her like he needed an answer.

"I was raised by my father. My mother died when I was young and he was very strict about certain things. Dating was not a priority in our house."

"Okay? What about in the last sixteen years since you left your house?"

She'd grown cold. Cut off and unemotional. It hurt her to have to acknowledge it and she was angry at Michael for forcing her to do so. "Why do you care about this?"

"Because I know you. I like you. I want to know you better but I keep running into this invisible wall and frankly, it's giving me a headache. So you screwed the president? Now that has to mean everything? Get on with your life."

"Get on with my life?" she shrieked. "Because it was what? A few thousand articles written in papers and magazines and online. Three or four books written by people who didn't even know me but who passed judgment on me. News stories and pictures and twenty-four-hour coverage for what…six months? Seven months. In America, in Europe. Hell, at one point the whole damn world was talking about it. People offered me thousands of dollars for the clothes I was wearing that night. A ten-thousand-dollar offer alone for my underwear, if you can believe it. But I mean, really, why dwell?"

"Hey," he said, softening his voice. "I didn't mean to upset you."

"No, Michael. You brought this up. You said it. You didn't want to have sex with Charlene. She didn't make your d-dick hard. You had that choice. You want to know why I haven't had sex with anyone in seven years?"

"Madeleine, don't…"

"Because I stopped having a choice. After it all came out…after the things the press said about me, men who knew me, who I thought knew me, suddenly believed me to be a very different type of woman. I couldn't be in a room alone with a man for five seconds without having to explain that no, I don't take my clothes off as soon as I say hello. Then came the men who didn't know me but wanted to bag the president's girl. Like I had some magic sexual powers that would turn them into world leaders. I had to back away from everyone because I couldn't trust anyone."

He moved around the table and took her hand. He didn't do anything with it, just held it and looked at her.

"Did anyone hurt you?"

"They all hurt me."

He shook his head. "Did any of them touch you?"

She could see the fury in his eyes along with a harnessed violence that reminded her he came from a very different world than she did.

"No, it wasn't like that. No one forced me, but no one saw anything other than a woman who would freely lift her skirt. I wasn't me anymore. I was this sexual prize. I hated it."

"I'm sorry those men did that to you."

Madeleine didn't know what to say but she felt an overwhelming sense of gratitude. That he cared. This man who barely knew her when so many men who were close to her in her life didn't.

Like her father and her brother.

"I'm not like them. In fact, I'm the opposite of them. I don't want sex with you…instead I want to know you. I want to be something to you. Not your employer. Not your project of the hour."

"I can't. I simply can't ever do that again."

"Not even friends? Friends, Madeleine. Two grown-up people who can make that choice. This job is only going to last what… a couple of more weeks? Then you won't be working for me. No rules would be broken. And if you wanted to we could maybe stay in touch. A call every once in a while. A visit here and there. Friends."

"Friends?" She couldn't help herself. She was suspicious of his motives. Why did this man need her as a friend?

"I'm lonely, Madeleine," he said as if he'd read her mind. "I have my work and I love it but lately it feels like something is missing. Maybe I'm tired of the endless Charlenes. I think I would rather be able to sit down and have a drink and talk."

She was tempted. So tempted. Because she was lonely, too. This evening, as strange as it had been, had also been nice.

"Think about it. We're still working together so take that time to get to know me. The real me. And let me get to know you. The real you."

"This is the real me. Everything you see is everything I am." Or at least all she would let herself be as far as he was concerned.

He smiled a little sadly. "I don't think so, Madeleine. I think you're hiding behind your business suits. I'm only asking you to undo a couple of buttons."

The thought of him undressing her sent a little shiver through her body. This was why she'd fought so hard to keep him at arm's length. The brutal truth was she was attracted to him. The first man in more than seven years to interest her and once again she was working for him.

Life could seriously be unfair.

"I can't think about…anything between us. Not until the job is over. It has to be that way for me."

"Okay. Then work quick and turn me into someone respectable."

"How about we shoot for less unrespectable." They both laughed and the tension between them dissipated.

He dropped her hand and she realized he had been holding it all this time.

"I'll leave you tonight but can we do breakfast tomorrow morning? I'll pick you up here."

"That's fine. We'll eat here in the room, though."

He opened his mouth as if to say something but stopped.

"Tomorrow," he told her. "Thanks for the drink and the company."

"Your dime."

With that, Madeleine watched him leave and heard the door close behind him. Michael Langdon wanted to be her friend. Crazy enough, she wanted his friendship, too.

HE WAS SORRY he had lied to her. Deception in any form could kill a relationship, but Michael didn't see any other way around it. She was too closed off. He needed some way to get over the walls she'd spent the past seven years shoring up.

He hit the button between the elevators and waited for the ding to announce one had arrived. Stepping inside, he reassured himself that it would only be another ten hours until he saw her again. But that felt like too much time apart.

Whatever this was, it was crazy. He'd never felt like this before. Never dreamed he would. Yet as he stepped off the elevator and headed for the lobby doors he knew that this thing between them was important. He had nothing to offer a woman like her except a whole lot of baggage, but stubbornly he couldn't drag himself away from what he wanted.

Michael handed the valet his stub and started pacing along the sidewalk as he waited for his car.

Yeah, he probably shouldn't have lied about the friends thing. Of course he wanted that but he also wanted something more. Maybe this was his chance to have a grown-up relationship with a woman. Something different. Something he'd never really had. He hadn't lied when he'd said he was tired of Charlene and others like her. He also hadn't lied when he'd said he didn't want Madeleine for sex. She was more important than that.

He didn't have a word for what he and Madeleine were going to be to one another, but he knew he needed her.

She was changing him. Not just his reputation, but changing him from the inside. He was starting to want things he'd never thought were important. Like companionship and having someone in the universe care how his day went. He had thought he didn't need those things, but maybe he'd been wrong. His vision of the future was suddenly shifting—the life he had thought he was going to have and the life he just might have were different. As long as Madeleine was with him.

He would lie, cheat and steal all over again to hold on to her.

Poor Madeleine. She didn't know who she was dealing with.

CHAPTER FIVE

"MADDY!"

Madeleine ducked her head a bit and adjusted her sunglasses, confident they covered most of her face as she approached the sidewalk café on Rodeo Drive. Her old friend and coworker was the only person she would ever let get away with calling her by the old nickname.

"You channeling Jackie O or what?"

"Peg," Madeleine said as she reached the table and kissed her friend on the cheek. "One might hope for a little discretion."

"From me? Then it has been too long since we've seen each other. Sit down. I've ordered you an appletini. You're going to love it."

She was going to hate it. She preferred wine to hard alcohol but there would be no convincing Peg. Since she was here to ask a favor, she made the politically correct decision to play along.

"Look at you." Peg ran her finger up and

down to indicate Madeleine's choice of ensemble. "Very southern California chic."

"At home I'm always in business suits and I'm never recognized. I didn't think I would see a lot of those out here so I wanted to blend."

Madeleine wore an expensive solid-blue top matched with white capris and flat sandals that really cost too much for anyone to justify but she did, anyway. When she'd bought them she'd felt slightly wicked. She paired the ensemble with a patterned scarf around her hair. And the big sunglasses made her feel sufficiently camouflaged.

"You look good. Real good. More relaxed. I would never say this to your face before… wait, actually, I would but I never got the chance to say it…you looked like hell back in the day. Too much pressure and too much stress is not good for the complexion."

"Back in the day" was code for the campaign trail. When Madeleine had been molding a man to be president and Peg had been working with the press to get the message out. After winning the election Peg stayed on for two more years as junior press secretary. She left when she was given the opportunity to be a producer on television's more popular newsmagazine show, *Sunday Night Hour*. Of course Peg had been upset for her when the scandal broke. They were friends. But not so outraged to leave her job. Not that Madeleine would have ever expected her to. When you worked so hard to make it to the top, quitting on moral grounds wasn't an option.

Quitting because you could land a much more lucrative deal in the private sector was completely understandable.

"I mean it," she continued. "You were skinny and drawn. I know what you did to make that guy president and I think you paid for it. Physically and emotionally. It's no wonder your decision-making skills sucked when the jerk put the moves on you. You were vulnerable and he knew it."

"It wasn't lack of sleep and a bad diet, Peg." If only Madeleine could have blamed it on such things. "It was flat-out stupidity. But I don't want to talk about that. I'm here to talk about my favor."

The waiter arrived with their drinks and Peg carefully lifted the martini glass so as to not spill a drop even as she waved her other hand for Madeleine to continue.

"I want you to feature someone on an upcoming episode."

Peg put the glass down. "Don't leave me in suspense."

"Michael Langdon."

"Michael Langdon? The race-car guy? With the white spiky hair and glasses."

"That was him. Yes. He has since become a car designer. Specialty stuff mostly, but now he's developed something new and innovative for the mass market. He's trying to partner with one of the major manufacturers to roll out his concept and to do that we're trying to change his image a bit so they'll think he's worth the risk."

Peg's smile was infectious. "You're working again."

Madeleine expected this. To delay she took a sip of her own drink. It was too sweet so she set it back down. "I've been working for the last five years."

"Don't give me that bull. I know what you've been doing for Ben and it looked a lot more like hiding than working. Speaking of Ben…how is he?"

"Fighting."

"Yeah, he would do that. When I heard he was sick and how serious it was, I thought if he dies it's going to be like God dying. He's connected to so many people in so many ways. Once we lose him all those connections will break apart and we'll all be left on our own."

"He's not gone yet." Madeleine tried to believe that his fight was stronger than his sickness. But the longer the treatments went on with no confirmation from the doctors that they were working, it was getting harder to do so.

"Right. Okay. Back to your real job. You're turning Michael Langdon into what? Not a political candidate."

"No. A serious person. Someone who is trustworthy."

Peg laughed. "Honey, the only thing serious about that guy is he's seriously hot."

"Michael Langdon is a respectable and solid businessman. He's an entrepreneur with creative new ideas for the auto industry. An environmentalist who's concerned about our dependence on foreign oil and believes his electric car can change that while also offering the average American an affordable option."

"Interesting. Keep going."

They were interrupted as the waiter came over to take their lunch order and as soon as he left Madeleine continued. "He's everything you want to see in a success story. Raised in poverty, turned to crime, paid his debt to society then reformed his life. He's built himself up on his talent and brains. Now he wants to give something back."

"And make money."

"Of course make money," Madeleine allowed. "But that doesn't mean he can't do both."

"What do you think about him? Gut feeling. Winner? Loser?"

Gut feeling was a game they used to play a lot in the past. Any time they were working with a candidate's adviser, or hiring staff or dealing with the media. Gut feeling was a simple up-or-down vote that encompassed everything. Good guy, bad guy. Smart guy, dumb guy. Winner, loser.

Madeleine's gut was completely convinced. Which wasn't like her. She used to be more cautious and make her decisions more logically, based on facts and statistics. Despite having very little of either, she believed he was who he said he was. She hoped her belief wasn't because she *wanted* him to be who he said he was. Because she wanted to be his friend. "Winner."

"Very interesting. Madeleine Kane thinks there is more to Michael Langdon than meets the eye. Well, hell, yes, I want to interview him. Do I get you, too?"

"Outside of a handful of people, which

now includes you, no one knows I'm working for him. And it will stay that way. Won't
it, Peg?"

Peg's lips twitched as the veiled threat registered and was acknowledged. Madeleine
held on to a lot of secrets for a lot of people.
Peg was among that number.

"My lips are sealed. Now let's talk fun
stuff. What are you doing tonight?"

"Nothing." The idea of maybe doing dinner and drinks with Peg appealed to her.
Michael would be at the Drearson party sur-
rounded by countless starlets. It would help
take her mind off what could be happening
with any one of them.

Of course, her concern was purely from a
professional perspective. She had to hope he
behaved himself according to the image they
were trying to project for him. Being seen
stumbling drunk outside the party with three
women on his arm would not help.

Although somehow that image, while
nearly iconic for him, didn't match up with
the man she knew. The man who told Charlene Merritt thanks, but no thanks.

"Great, then we're going to a party."

"What party?"

"The hottest one in town. Academy-Award-winning director and producer Tom Drear-son."

Madeleine nearly snorted. "I'm so not going to that party."

"Why not?"

"Hello? Everyone in town is going to be there. Including Michael Langdon. It's why I got him an invitation. There will be a ton of press and coverage."

Peg rolled her eyes. "Yes, for real stars. Not us. Drearson always has a backdoor path available for the people who want to bypass the crowds. In the past there has been a famous actor or two who preferred to keep the sexual orientation of his date confidential. And then there is us, the people who the press couldn't care less about. Trust me, no one will see us and once we're inside there is no media at all."

Madeleine found herself hedging. When was the last time she'd been to a party like that?

Easy answer. Seven years ago. Seven years, when it all came crashing down and she'd stopped living.

She wasn't sure what was happening to her. Maybe it was Ben getting sick, or maybe she was flat-out bored. Or maybe it was meeting Michael and feeling excited about something again. But she was feeling restless. Like she couldn't stay inside her skin anymore.

Seven years…maybe it was time to accept her self-appointed sentence in solitary confinement might finally be up. But just because she could mentally tell herself that there was nothing wrong with attending a party, that didn't mean she could actually summon up the courage to go.

"Come on. You know you want to."

She did want to. Like she'd wanted to sit with Michael and have a glass of wine. But she was starting to sense a dangerous pattern. As if maybe the rules were no longer working because she was tired of following them. She felt like a dieter who had gone too long only eating carrot sticks and suddenly wanted a slice of cake. The temptation was almost impossible to resist.

"You really promise me that we can get in without being seen?"

"Madeleine, I hate to break it to you, but even if you were seen, I'm not sure anyone would care. I mean, really, all that scandal stuff died years ago. How long has it been?"

"Seven years." The number resonated in her head like a gong going off as it counted out seven beats.

"In the world of today's media that's a lifetime ago."

"I don't want to take any chances."

"We can get in without being seen," Peg assured her. "You can always wear your camouflage gear as a backup plan."

Madeleine fidgeted with her sunglasses. One drink with Michael hadn't resulted in them tumbling into bed. One party shouldn't hurt, either. And damn it, she really wanted that slice of cake. "Okay. I'm in. What time?"

"Nineish?"

Madeleine took a deep breath as their food arrived. "Well, then, we better carb up now because I'm going to need a dress and I can't think of a better place to look than on Rodeo Drive, can you?"

"Ooooh," Peg groaned. "Look out *Pretty Woman,* here we come."

MICHAEL TILTED HIS head lower to hear what the woman was saying. He was almost convinced she was whispering so he would have to bend his body closer to her. That thought was confirmed when she ran her hand over his neck and in his hair.

"You want to take me home?"

Michael pulled away from the young

blonde thing with the large plastic breasts. "We were just introduced."

Like that mattered in Hollywood. He had money. He had connections, otherwise he wouldn't have gotten an invitation to this party, and she wanted to use her body and pretty face to her best advantage.

"So?"

"Exactly. If you'll excuse me, I need another drink."

He walked away without offering to fetch her one and knew he was being rude. In the past couple of weeks, on his grand tour of respectability, he had imagined how a gentleman might behave, how Madeleine would expect a gentleman to behave—and then tried to be that person. Walking abruptly away from the woman was decidedly unlike that person.

He never would have walked away from Madeleine.

On his way through the crowd toward one of the five bars that had been set up on the perimeter of the patio, Michael stopped.

It was like he summoned her out of thin air. His very own party angel.

Amongst the starlets she stood out like the North Star. Where they sparkled and glittered and showed off their skin and cleavage she stood brighter and more solid in a simple black dress that reflected elegance and class. She was the queen in a land of fairy princesses.

That feeling of being drawn to her flooded him. If he looked too long and too hard at her he might never be able to look away again. His brain screamed that he wanted her so loud that he wondered if he wasn't actually shouting out to everyone around him.

No one moved or turned, so he imagined he was safe. No, she couldn't have heard him because she started to walk toward him.

"Hi."

The simple greeting snapped him out of his crazy thoughts.

"Hi. This is a surprise. If I thought for a second you would come to something like this I would have invited you."

"But you know I would never have come with you…at least not as your date. I sort of snuck in the back door. No photographers." Madeleine pointed over her shoulder to an overly tall woman with glasses, standing at the bar. "Peg Neely got me in. She's my contact at *Sunday Night Hour.* She wants to meet you. If she likes your story she's agreed to consider doing a feature on you for the show."

When she'd run the idea by him the first

time he hadn't been crazy about it. Those types of news shows did their homework. While his prison record was common knowledge there were other areas of his life he didn't want people digging in too closely.

For the most part, Michael had cleaned up any loose ends that had to do with his time in prison. Money was a powerful motivator for people to keep quiet.

Still there could be stragglers.

Since he didn't want to communicate any of the reasons for his reluctance to Madeleine he decided to let her go ahead and try. Just because she was going to pitch him as an interview didn't mean they would accept the idea.

He'd forgotten how incredibly good she was at her job.

"You're sure this is the right track?" he hedged.

"I'm positive. You told me on the flight out here that your people were getting better responses from the CEOs regarding a partnership. No one is dismissing you outright, which is a start. You take your passion and put it out front on the national stage, it should seal the deal."

"Because of you."

Madeleine shook her head. "Because of you. Come meet Peg. You'll like her."

He took her arm to stop her from leaving. He liked holding her. Any part of her. "You know about my past."

"Of course. I can't imagine spending any length of time in prison can be considered a good thing, but it does add to your narrative."

He let go of her arm. It added to his narrative. He'd never heard it described that way before.

Instantly Madeleine reached out and squeezed his hand. "Hey, I'm sorry. That was so insensitive of me. I used to do it all the time. Trivialize people's harsh realities when I was putting them in the context of a picture I was trying to create. I once told the president he looked like a mean version of Mr. Rogers anytime he wore sweaters and that he probably frightened children."

Michael laughed and watched the expression on Madeleine's face change. She had started to laugh with him but quickly realized what she was laughing about and stopped.

"That's the first time you've done that, isn't it? Talk about him as a fond memory."

She met his eyes and he could see the answer in them. "Yes. I try so hard to not think about…him at all. But it slipped out."

Michael thought that was a good thing. It meant on some level she trusted him. He liked the idea of her trusting him because it was how he would start finding a way around those boundaries of hers.

He could see her thinking about it too much, so he changed the topic.

"Come dance with me."

A band and a dance floor had been constructed on another level of the backyard area. Michael could hear the music drifting over the sounds of conversation. It was a risky thing, bringing her close, holding her in his arms. But the idea latched on and wouldn't let go.

She was already shaking her head. "I don't think..."

"Nothing can happen on a dance floor, Madeleine." He took a step closer and realized she was still holding his hand, hadn't let it go all this time—and still didn't even as he moved closer. "All we can do is sway back and forth to the music. Nothing dangerous about that."

"People would see."

"People would see two people dancing. Most people don't even know who I am without my white spiky hair. And you, in that dress, with your hair loose around your shoulders, you don't look like Madeleine Kane."

"No?"

"No. You'll put your arm around my waist. If you want you can rest your head on my shoulder…"

Her eyes narrowed slightly. "Is that what friends do when they dance?"

"I don't know. I've never danced with a friend. I would like to try. With you."

"Michael…I don't…"

"What have we here?" The tall woman with the glasses and the long face approached them. "Is Maddy actually touching another human being?"

Instantly Madeleine dropped his hand and backed away. Michael instantly disliked the woman who approached them.

"Peg, this is Michael. Michael, Peg Neely. She worked for the press secretary during the Marlin administration and now is a producer for *Sunday Night Hour*."

The woman, who was older than Madeleine by a few years, stuck out her hand. "I hear you're creating a car that's going to save the world."

"Save the world might be a reach. Save people a few bucks on gas sounds more like it."

"Ah, but that's not as television-worthy."

Peg looked him up and down and he felt himself being assessed. Like he was the car and she was kicking the tires and lifting the hood. He felt naked and didn't like it. Holding out his arms he spun around, then opened up the button on his sport coat and spread it wide.

"Well, am I television-worthy or not? You want me to take off my shirt? Drop my pants?" He reached for the buckle at his waist.

"Michael!" Madeleine said, clearly confused by his behavior.

"Oooh…he's got some teeth. I like it. Yes, Mr. Langdon, I think you are absolutely television-worthy. Are you ready to open up to the American public? I'm warning you, my researchers will have full rein to dig into every corner of your life and if it's something I think the people need to know then whoever we pick to conduct the interview won't pull any punches."

"I can take a few hits."

It would be fine, he thought. What were the odds that some researcher would find any stragglers from prison who might have something to say about him? And if he did the interview it wasn't like he had to worry about any former inmates deciding to come track him down.

After all, they didn't get to watch *Sunday Night Hour* in prison.

CHAPTER SIX

A FEW DAYS later, Madeleine found herself back in Detroit doing what she promised herself she wouldn't do. Couldn't do. But it seemed to be happening without her consent. She was succumbing to Michael's irresistible aura.

It was as if she was standing on a pair of heavily waxed skis and finding it impossible to stop the slide down a snow-covered mountain. Of course, she'd put herself on the mountain and she wasn't sure if that made her a masochist or not.

He was everything she'd ever believed a man could be. A perfect blend of intelligence and ambition, mixed with compassion and sweetness. Intensity mixed with humor. Confidence mixed with a shyness she detected from time to time.

They were sitting side by side at a picnic table covered with a red-and-white-checkered plastic cloth, wrist deep in the most delicious barbecue sauce she'd ever tasted. Michael was telling stories about racing in Europe that made his friend Archie, who was sitting across the table, light up like a Christmas tree.

How could she not fall for this man?

More importantly, how was she going to stop it?

It had taken a major effort on his part to get her to come out in public with him today but in the end Michael's arguments had convinced her. They were going to a place that was sure to be free of any and all media and her anonymity could be guaranteed. And after making it through the party in L.A. without anyone recognizing her, she was feeling slightly bolder and a little more daring.

Everything Michael had said about the place was true. Darnell's small outdoor barbecue joint wasn't a place she was going to have to worry about running into photographers. She felt safe here. The fact that they were currently the only customers helped even more.

Besides, Archie was someone she had really wanted to meet. He was an important part of Michael's life and getting to know his old friend would mean getting to know Michael better.

Michael had talked nonstop about Archie on the ride over to Darnell's, and she could sense when he talked about him he was talking about family. Within minutes of meeting Archie she was instantly charmed by the old flirt.

She also could see what he'd given back to Michael when Archie took the ex-con under his wing. Archie Beeker's innate goodness and generosity clearly allowed Michael to free himself from the foul stink of prison and find a new purpose in his life. She would be forever grateful to the old man. And if Michael's car turned out to be the sensation she knew it could be, the world might find itself indebted to one Archie Beeker.

"...the tire is as flat as a pancake and I'm watching as Jean Claude whizzes by me with his finger out the window."

Archie laughed then stopped himself. "Hey, you shouldn't be saying things like that in front of the lady here."

Archie said the word *lady* as if she was royalty, but when she had her mouth wrapped around a rib and sauce was smeared from ear to ear she didn't feel so ladylike.

"I didn't say which finger," Michael allowed.

Madeleine giggled and set the now-clean bone on the plate.

"What do you say, Mickey," Darnell shouted from beside his massive barbecue pit, "you need another plate of ribs? Your woman over there seems to have quite a hunger." He was stoking the pit with hickory wood and basting various cuts of meat with his secret sauce.

Madeleine tried to pretend she didn't hear him call her Michael's "woman." As a rational, independent woman in her thirties such a description should have offended her.

Instead it thrilled her.

She was such a goner. What the hell was she going to do?

"Nah, I think we're done, Darnell." Michael was looking at Madeleine when he said it. "I let her eat any more of your food and she's never going to want to go home."

"That is a very true statement," Madeleine said as she reached for the wipes. She got a good start on her fingers before moving on to her face.

Darnell must have felt encouraged because he continued, "I like a woman who knows how to eat. Them skinny ones might be pretty to look at but they're hard all over in bed. You hearin' me, Mickey?"

Michael ducked his head to avoid looking at Madeleine. "You trying to get fresh with my girl, Darnell, because I will have words with you."

Darnell was six feet five inches of solid muscle honed by lifting so many animal carcasses daily. Yet Madeleine had no doubt Michael would charge to her rescue if he thought she needed it. No, he wouldn't hesitate for a second. One more thing for her to feel gooey about.

Fortunately, Darnell simply laughed and continued slapping on the sauce.

"This was good. It's good to see you have fun," Archie said. Then he reached out and cuffed Michael gently on the back of the head. "What did I tell you, you need more of this and less work all the time."

Madeleine started to say that technically they were still working. The day's outing, through his favorite spots in Detroit, was only about showing her all the sides of himself so she would better understand him. In theory, this would help her do her job better by making sure she was highlighting his best elements to the press.

She couldn't even make herself believe it.

"He's a hard worker," Archie said to her.

"Which is a good thing. But sometimes everyone needs a break."

Madeleine nodded, feeling the older man's words resonate inside her. "I agree, Archie. Here, you've got some sauce on your ear."

Madeleine leaned over the table and wiped the older man's ear with the towelette.

"I like you. You got class, anyone can see. But you can still eat with your fingers like a real person. Yeah, you're gold. I like this one, Michael."

"Am I going to have to fight you off, too? Get your own date."

Archie laughed as he put his hands on the table and made to stand. "I got to get back to the shop. That new project I told you about. You're going to come in and meet him, right? Just a hello or something."

Sitting next to Michael, Madeleine could feel his body stiffen all over.

"Sure. I said I would, Archie. How about tomorrow?"

"That's fine. He's doing all right. Doesn't have your fire, though. Hopefully he can keep working enough to get his life back on track."

"If he's working with you he's got a shot."

"You're a good kid. And you're a nice lady. Here, what do I owe for my half of the food?"

"You know your money is no good with Darnell. He won't take a dime. Save it and maybe get a haircut, old man. I can see you got hair sprouting out your ears."

Archie snarled, but covered his ears. "You wait. Someday you're going to be an old man and you'll see where the hair you don't want grows."

Archie left and Michael pulled out some cash from his wallet and threw it down on the table.

"Did I see cash? I don't want to see no cash on that table, Mickey. You know your money is no good here."

"Darnell, relax. It's a tip for your girl for doing the serving. You want me to stiff her?"

"I guess that's all right. You come back around again soon, now. I'm trying out a new brisket rub."

"Will do."

Michael led Madeleine back to the street where his car was parked.

"That was a generous tip," Madeleine noted. He'd left a hundred dollar bill for the girl.

"I helped Darnell out with a loan a couple of years ago when he wanted to fix up the outside so he could add more tables. Now he doesn't take my money. But Tamara is saving for college so I like to slip her extra when I can."

"He calls you Mickey."

"He knew me from before."

Before. It must be exactly that way for him. Before prison and after.

"Is it hard to hear that name? Does it remind you of too much?" She wasn't sure why she was asking. If it did bother him, it was like intentionally poking at a sore tooth.

"It reminds me of who I was. Which isn't a bad thing sometimes. You forget where you came from and you start taking things easy. Next thing you know, you're sliding backward."

"Afraid you're going to end up stealing cars again?"

"No. Just afraid I won't remember I was once a kid who stole cars. If that happens I'll start taking everything I've built for granted."

They reached the car and he held the door open for Madeleine. She was anxious to ask where they were going next but wouldn't let herself for fear of his answer. After all, they had spent the whole day together. No doubt he wanted to drop her off at the hotel. It was a Saturday, but he might need to go back into the office. A man who owned his own company didn't often get the luxury of a weekend.

Sure enough, his phone rang and listening to his side of the conversation she could tell it was one of his engineers. He was probably needed and their day was about to come to an end.

She would not be disappointed. She would not.

"That's great. Yes. Absolutely. I'm on my way over." Michael ended the call and looked at her with a gleam in his eye. "You got time for me to show you one more thing?"

"Sure." She hoped that sounded casual because she didn't feel casual at all.

They drove for a time and Madeleine realized they were heading out of the city. She must have been fidgeting or maybe watching for signs because he smiled at her and wiggled his eyebrows.

"Don't get nervous. My business offices are in downtown, but my factory is outside of the city. Closer to where I live in Grosse Pointe."

"I didn't think you were kidnapping me." But she did think he was taking her to his home and that had made her nervous. Once she was inside his home it would be official. They would know each other on a personal level. And she had already broken so many rules.

His home was far away from where someone might see them, so anything might happen. And that final rule about never, ever getting involved with someone she worked with might also be in jeopardy.

Madeleine closed her eyes and tried to remind herself of everything she had lost the last time she had listened to a man tell her that no one would ever find out about them. Unfortunately, as easy as it was to recall the memory and remind her of her deep shame, it was also easy to see how this time things were different.

Her job with him was only temporary.

He wasn't married.

Two points that made what she did the last time unforgivably stupid.

But what was she even thinking about doing? He hadn't once asked her to his home in the past few weeks. He hadn't tried to kiss or seduce her. He'd said he wanted to be friends and he hadn't offered anything more than that.

Yes, he'd asked her to dance at the party in California. She thought she had seen in his expression an offer for something more than friendship. But after she had refused and they had spoken with Peg, he hadn't asked her again.

He also hadn't left her side at all that evening. They ate and drank and got starstruck together as various Hollywood royalty strutted about. They'd had fun. At the end of the night he'd taken her back to her hotel and left her with nothing more than a soft kiss on the cheek.

A friendly peck and nothing more.

So wondering if he was taking her to his home so he could ravish her was a fairly ridiculous thought.

He made a turn into what appeared to be a complex with multiple buildings. The property was fenced off with a guard on duty. Michael pulled up to the gate and waited as the uniformed guard came forward. Michael offered his identification and then put his thumb on what appeared to be a tablet. After a beep, he pulled his hand back.

"And the lady, sir?"

"It's okay, Walt. She's with me."

"Yes, sir."

The man stepped back and the gate opened.

"Very high tech," Madeleine noted.

"Not really. It's pretty standard. We had the bare minimum before, but after I started working on the new design I beefed things up. I want to partner up with one of the bigger companies and take my fair share of the profits, not have them take my idea and bring it to the market themselves."

"I have to imagine most of those big companies are already working on an all-electric model. There are some currently available."

Michael nodded as he pulled his car up next to the largest building in the complex, which looked to Madeleine like an airplane hangar. "Sure they are. But my car is different and everyone is going to want one. You'll see. It's Saturday, so only Craig and a skeleton crew will be around. I'll warn you ahead of time Craig is a really intense guy when he's focused on the work. Don't take offense if he doesn't acknowledge you."

Madeleine got out and followed him to an entrance. This door required a security code, then once inside there was another door requiring his thumb scan again. When that door opened they walked into a massive area filled with too many electronic equipment, computers and robotics to fully take in. It looked like something out of a futuristic movie.

"Wow," she muttered.

"I know. Right. I call this my Pimp Garage."

A few people bustled about and Michael waved in their general direction.

In the center of the room was a raised platform and on that sat a very nondescript silver vehicle. On the platform with it was a man wearing a casual pair of jeans and a sweatshirt and tapping away on his computer tablet.

"Craig!"

The man turned and waved. His hair was a mess where he'd obviously been running his hands through it. He was older than Michael, maybe by a decade, and when he hopped off the platform to greet them he stumbled.

He was clearly not an athlete, but coordination wasn't exactly necessary for programming.

"Michael, check this out. She's fully operational. I finished some of the last testing early this morning. I couldn't wait until Monday to show you."

As they approached the man stopped as he took note of Madeleine's presence.

"Who is she?"

"Craig, this is Madeleine Kane. She's been helping me revamp my image in the media so hopefully someone will take me seriously as a partner."

He eyed her suspiciously. "How do we know she's not a spy?"

Michael turned to her. "Excellent question. Are you a spy?"

Madeleine knew he was teasing but the idea was so absurd she had to respond. "Don't be ridiculous. Spies are fairly anonymous people. I don't quite fit the mold."

"Oh," Craig said as if remembering where he'd heard her name before. "That's right, you're the president's girl. The one he got caught banging."

Michael snarled. "Madeleine is currently in my employment and as such should be treated with all due respect."

"Don't worry about it," Madeleine said coolly. "There wasn't anything you said that wasn't fact."

"It's not all right," Michael said tightly.

"Michael, please," she insisted, wanting to end this conversation as quickly as possible. "We're here to see the car. I'm sure he didn't mean anything by it."

He looked at her then and after a moment let it go. "Fine."

"Look, I'm sorry. But the car—you're going to love it." Craig handed Michael the tablet. "Typically you would use the earpiece. But for showman's sake I've got her on Speaker. Okay. Turn her on."

"Good afternoon, Irene," Michael said, addressing the car.

"Good afternoon, Michael."

Madeleine gasped. The car had spoken back.

"Activate car. Driver side and front passenger-side door open. Temperature set to seventy degrees and radio off."

Madeleine understood that the direction was being communicated to the tablet and then the commands were being directed to the car, but watching the car come to life and the doors pop open was remarkable.

"The idea is to use your smartphone to talk to your car. The computer systems will be fully integrated. Your music, your contact lists, all of it. Most remote starters have to be within a certain periphery to work, but not mine. From your home, or office or wherever you are, you can set the temperature in advance so it's either heated or cooled accordingly."

"Very cool."

Michael hopped onto the platform and reached for her hand. The platform was only about two feet off the ground and required a really big step, but his strength lifted her off her feet so that she stumbled against him.

He didn't seem to be affected by their contact and kept talking while he circled the vehicle. "It has total voice recognition, which makes theft all but impossible. Not to mention it keeps teenagers from taking Mom and Dad's car without permission. You can program the voice you would like to hear and really communicate with it. There is total voice control over all functionality within the car as well as over your phone." His voice grew more animated with each feature he described. "You can talk out a text, or make a call or tell it to find a music station you like. It has all the most innovative safety features to alert drivers if they drift off the road or something runs in front of them."

It was amazing. He was amazing. He rattled off how it was powered up, how long the charge lasted and how fast it could go. But Madeleine wasn't hearing any of it.

All she could think of was how big this was going to be for him. His excitement was contagious. She could see the passion and determination in his eyes and his whole body as he pointed at each new gadget. It was doing fluttery things to her insides.

Then she thought about what it all meant. The end game was to bring this car to the public and she could see now why he knew it would be a success. Something this cool at an affordable price, of course people were going to want it.

Which meant Michael Langdon was about to become more popular and well-known than Steve Jobs and Bill Gates put together. The nation's spotlight was about to turn on him in a major way.

And the spotlight was a place she would never go back to.

"COME TO dinner with me."

He had insisted on walking her up to her hotel room and was now standing inside the room with his body holding the door open like he didn't want to leave.

"Michael, we've spent the whole day together. You're no doubt sick of my company."

"I'm not. Come to dinner with me."

She sighed. "You know I won't do that."

"You ate lunch with me at Darnell's."

"That was different. It was just us and Archie. Besides, I'm feeling tired. I don't know that I would be good company."

Michael stepped inside and let the hotel door close behind him. "This is because of what Craig said, isn't it? You've been different since then. More withdrawn."

The distance she knew she was exuding wasn't because of what Michael's engineer said. She was still thinking about how she was going to stop herself from doing something utterly stupid, like fall for Michael Langdon.

"I should have… When he said that, I should have done something. Fired him, I don't know."

"Fired him? He's your head engineer," Madeleine said to inject some reason into the conversation. She kicked off her shoes and didn't let herself think about how comfortable she'd become with him. It didn't even bother her that they were alone together in her room or that she no longer cared if he saw her without her shoes. "Michael, it was a comment. It happens when people meet me for the first time. They look at me for a second with that I-think-she-looks-familiar gaze and then it's, 'You're not *that* Madeleine Kane, are you?'"

"I didn't defend you the way you deserve."

She walked over to him, grabbed his hand, squeezing it to show her gratitude. "That's sweet, but I don't need you to defend me. Remember, I was sort of the guilty party in that very sordid play."

"Bullshit. He was the one who was married. The more I've come to know you, the more it makes me sick to think what happened to you. All the scandal, all the jokes, all the trash that came down on you. You, the least slutty person I know. How people couldn't see that about you, I don't know."

Madeleine swallowed as a rush of guilt welled up again even after all these years. She turned her back to him. "I wasn't innocent."

"How can you say that? You ooze moral uprightness and goodness. Sure, maybe you made a mistake. Maybe the most powerful man on the planet talked his way into your panties, but you can't be blamed for that."

It was his outrage on her behalf that got to her. She had to stop it. It wasn't right for her to let him go on thinking she was blameless. It wasn't right for him to want to defend her when she wasn't the heroine in this story.

"You don't know everything about me," she said, facing him again.

"Then tell me. Because that's what I want to know. Everything."

She could see how serious he was. "Maybe you won't like me so much after you know the truth."

"Try me."

His assurance humbled her. His deep-rooted certainty that she was innocent and good and couldn't have done the thing everyone accused her of doing, it made her feel covered with grime. Maybe it was best that she told him. Maybe when he saw her, finally saw who she was, he would be the one to pull back, and she wouldn't have to worry about her feelings for him anymore.

"I told you my mother died and my father raised me."

"Yes. I'm sorry, by the way. I don't know if I said that."

"She had cancer. It was very hard for a while. After she was gone, it was just my father and my brother. They expected things from me. Expected me to work hard, excel and behave. I went to an all-girl high school. I received top grades and honors. I was accepted into Yale where again I received top grades and honors. My first job was for a state senate campaign and I distinguished myself quickly in political circles. I worked three more elections and in each of those, my candidate won. When Jason Marlin asked me to be part of the team, I leaped at the chance to take my game to the national level. My father was thrilled. Proud. My brother was jealous and that was almost as satisfying."

"You don't have to do this," he said abruptly. "I don't want you to have to talk about this if you don't want to."

"No. You wanted the truth and this is it. Anyway, it should have been an amazing time. I was on top of the world. Then things started to change. I started to resent the president almost immediately after the election. Something shifted in him as soon as he won. In hindsight, I can say maybe it's something all candidates experience when they win. They have to transition from someone running for office to a leader. Suddenly my advice—which had been so pivotal in winning the election—was not as necessary once he had the job."

"But he made you a senior adviser."

"Which many in the old guard of the party resented. I was too young. Too inexperienced. I was no longer as useful as I once was. No longer important."

"I bet that ticked you off."

"I nearly hated him."

"Then how did it happen?"

Madeleine closed her eyes. Every day of her life since it did, she asked herself the same question.

"He'd never done anything overtly aggressive on the campaign but I always knew by the way he watched me. The times his hand would linger on my back. Or the way he would stare at me for too long. My experience with sex before that…well, let's say I wasn't the most experienced. But I wasn't naive. I knew what he wanted."

She took a breath and considered what she was doing. What she was about to say, she had never said to anyone. So why was she telling Michael, the one man whose opinion suddenly mattered so much to her?

"Go on," he encouraged. "It's okay. I'm not going to judge."

Maybe that's why she was telling him. Maybe deep down she knew that out of anyone, he might understand. After all, he had also made mistakes.

"One night, it was the two of us alone in the Oval. I was arguing a point on an upcoming social-security reform bill Congress was about to put up for a vote and he wasn't listening. He wasn't listening to me. And suddenly I snapped. I asked him if he wanted to have sex with me. I thought at least in this I would have control."

Sitting on the couch, she leaned forward and dropped her face in her hands. It was too hard to look at him. Too hard to say it while he was watching her. But she had to finish it. This was the ugly truth and it was what she'd promised him. She couldn't hide from it. Sitting straighter, she promised herself she wouldn't cry. She didn't deserve any sympathy for what she'd done.

"While it was happening, all I could think of was how bad I was. Not a good girl anymore. If my father saw what I was doing, how horrified he would be. No, sir, I was a woman who could make a president get down on his knees if I wanted. Then his wife walked in and the world knows the rest of the story."

"You've never told anyone that before, have you? You didn't have to tell me."

"I know. But I wanted you to know. I wanted you to know that when all those disgusting stories were being written about me, every one of them was true. I wasn't some poor young woman who was taken advantage of like some people tried to portray me. My friends all thought I had been seduced or tricked. And the whole time I knew it was me. I made that decision. He might never have acted on his feelings if I hadn't opened the door for him."

"Don't…"

"No, I knew what I was doing, and it wasn't out of affection or even attraction. I wanted payment. I wanted to be listened to again. You know what that makes me?"

"Don't say it."

"A whore." She gulped as the word rose up like bile in her throat, burning along the way.

"Stop it," he barked. "I won't let anyone talk about you like that. I sure as shit am not going to listen to you say it about yourself."

"It's the truth."

"It's you beating yourself up for a mistake you made seven years ago. You messed up. You suffered for it. Move on."

He didn't understand. He was blinded by something—exactly what, she didn't know—but there was no justifying her actions. She didn't deserve his defense.

"I can't. So no, I don't want to go to dinner with you. And maybe now you'll understand why I can't let it go. Why I'll never let it go. Because everything that happened…it was all my fault."

CHAPTER SEVEN

"HEY, ARCHIE! You here?" Michael called into the open garage, thinking he'd find Archie and his new project busy at work. He'd picked today to come by since he found himself alone. Madeleine had gone back to Philadelphia to tie up some loose ends on a job and check on Ben. At least that's what she'd said. She insisted it wasn't because she was running from him.

He had to trust that she was telling the truth. And trust that she was coming back.

Instead of finding Archie and his project, the place seemed almost empty except for an old banged-up Chevy. Then a man slid out from underneath the car with some grease stains lining his face.

"Archie ain't here. He went out to the bank."

Michael waited for the guy to sit up to introduce himself and when he did it was like a punch in his gut. The man wasn't much to look at. Short, thin, partially balding with small eyes that dipped into his head. But despite the years and the grease, the recognition was instantaneous. Archie's new project wasn't a stranger.

The man got off the glide and then walked over to a worktable looking for a clean rag he could use on his hands. He had barely acknowledged Michael's presence and Michael wondered if he could somehow back out of the garage without having to engage him. But then he could feel eyes on him, sizing him up.

"Hey, I know you."

Too late. "I'm sorry," Michael muttered. "I don't—"

"It's me. Nooky Clarke. You're Mickey Lang. I was in the cell next to you at Wayne County, like, fifteen years ago."

"I don't think so—"

"Oh, wow, you're the guy Archie was talking about. The one who made out driving cars and shit. I didn't put it together. Michael Langdon. Mickey Lang. Go figure, right?"

Michael tried to swallow the acid that was filling his mouth. He didn't want to see this man. Didn't want to acknowledge he knew him. "I came by because…Archie's a friend."

"You really don't remember me? Most guys I know, they don't forget much about their time inside. It's one of those things that stick, if you know what I mean."

"I can promise you I've forgotten all of it," Michael said softly. At least almost all of it. "Look, just let Archie know I was here."

"Sure thing. And hey, if you've got any fancy car problems, I know how to change oil and shit now."

"Thanks." Michael turned and forced himself to not give in to the urge to run out of the shop screaming but to take each step slowly and deliberately. After all, it wasn't like you could outrun the past.

"Congrats and all on making it big. You know, the money and stuff." Nooky was still talking even as Michael walked away. Still standing in the garage rubbing his hands with a rag that was no longer clean. "When Archie told me about this fancy ex-con I was like, eff that. I don't need no pep talk from some rich dude. But I remember you, Mickey. Yeah, I remember you real good."

Trying not to hear anything ominous in the man's tone, Michael finally did the grown-up thing and turned around. He didn't have a pep talk in him, but the least he could do was offer the man some truth. "If you keep your nose clean, Archie can do right by you."

"Like he did for you?"

Michael swallowed again, this time more with sentiment than disgust. "Yeah, yeah, like he did for me."

"Be seeing you around, Mickey." The man raised the greasy rag in his hand like some kind of flag salute.

Michael didn't say it, but under his breath he whispered, "I hope not."

READY TO LEAVE Philadelphia and head back to Detroit, Madeleine wasn't pleased with the weather slowing her down. Rain poured down as she made her way from the cab to Ben's front door. Madeleine cursed under her breath. Her plan was to visit Ben one last time and then head directly to the airport.

The cabdriver had pulled up as far as he could on the driveway, but even during her sprint up the short path to Ben's front door she'd felt the rain soak through her sweater to her skin. The thought of sitting on the plane soaking wet didn't appeal to her much.

She should cancel her flight.

She squashed the thought as soon as it came to her. She couldn't cancel a flight because of some damp clothes. And she couldn't cancel her flight because, while going back and seeing Michael again after everything she had told him was going to be hard, in the end she was a professional and a professional finished the job.

Michael wanted her to come back. He wanted to discuss the upcoming green-initiative marathon she had scheduled him to speak at.

Madeleine wasn't stupid. She strongly suspected his need to have her by his side was his way of proving to her she hadn't disgusted him with her confession. She wasn't sure why. She disgusted herself every time she thought about what she'd done.

But Michael was insistent. He hadn't been happy at all when she'd told him she was returning to Philadelphia. She had to assure him it was only temporary to finish up some details from her last assignment and to check on Ben. Only then did he seem mollified.

It wasn't lost on her that if she chose not to return, it would be easier to deal with Michael remotely rather than in person. But duty won out over embarrassment, so she was going back. She refused to acknowledge the small kernel of excitement living in her heart, knowing she was going to be seeing him again that afternoon.

She rang the bell a few times and tried to huddle under the overhang that only kept her partially dry since the wind was blowing rain everywhere. One more reason to hate spring, in her opinion. One day it could be mild and hinting of warmer days to come, the next you were being soaked by a cold, dreary rain.

She could see Anna's car in the driveway so she knew they were both home. She didn't imagine she would be interrupting anything and wanted to see Ben before heading back to Detroit. After a minute with no answer, she took the initiative and pulled out her key ring. Ben had given her a spare some time ago because he'd been spending more and more time working from his home rather than coming into the office.

Once inside the foyer, she opened her mouth to announce herself but stopped when she heard shouting.

"What the hell are you talking about? What do you mean it's none of my concern? You can say that? After what happened?"

It was Anna's voice and she was upset. No, she was angry.

"Don't tell me how I feel. Don't you dare!"

Madeleine was stunned. In the years she'd known Anna and Ben she'd never heard anything more than playful banter between them. Yes, they teased and mocked one another ruthlessly, but never with any real heat.

This wasn't banter. This was a fight.

"You want me to leave? You want me to quit? Tell me. Just say one damn thing that's the truth!"

Madeleine couldn't hear any of Ben's side of the conversation. Not that it surprised her. Raising his voice would be intolerable to him. He was always measured and careful in everything he said. Plus, given his weakened condition, it was quite possible he didn't have the strength to shout back.

It was his condition that forced Madeleine into motion. Anna might be angry with good reason, but Ben wasn't in a position to fight back and that wasn't fair.

"Hello! Ben? Anna?" She was loud enough to get their attention. She could tell from the direction of Anna's voice they were in Ben's office so she headed down the foyer to the room on the left.

The sliding door was halfway open, and with another shove she pushed it aside to let herself in. "Hey, sorry. I rang, but there was no answer so I used my key."

Anna stood with arms crossed over her chest, her face a picture of restrained fury. Upon seeing Madeleine, though, she quickly altered her tone. "Hi, Madeleine. Sorry, we were just…talking. I'll let you visit while I take care of some things." She turned back to Ben, who was leaning against the fireplace, not looking at either woman. "We're not through with this."

"Anna, we most decidedly are. Please leave us."

Once more Madeleine was stunned. The dismissal in his tone was like nothing she'd ever heard from him. That he could use it with Anna, who had been everything to him in these past months since he'd been diagnosed, was even more bizarre.

The door slid shut with a thump and they were alone.

"Ben?"

"Don't. Please. I'm begging you not to ask."

Madeleine shifted on her feet. Hearing Ben beg for anything was nearly as awful as his dismissal of Anna. Without question she would respect his wishes. But she had no intention of leaving without talking to Anna first. "Okay. I'm sorry I interrupted."

"I'm not. It wasn't a conversation I wanted to have," he said as he made his way to his desk. Though he didn't shake or stumble, she could see the effort it required for him to move across the room and take his seat.

"How are you?"

"I suck. Leukemia has that effect on a person. But I don't want to talk about that, either. Tell me how things are going with you and Michael."

"Going with us? What's that supposed to mean?"

"It means are you being successful at your job?" he asked carefully.

Too late, Madeleine realized her reaction had been defensive.

"Yes, things are good. I think we're going to get the *Sunday Night Hour* interview. Once people are able to see what he's talking about and understand his vision, I think there will be partners lined up around the corner ready to do business with him. Former reputation or not."

"Excellent. Then you'll be coming home soon."

Madeleine ignored the knot in her stomach. "Yes. Soon. He won't have much more need for my services."

"Job well done, then. When you return, there is a state senate campaign in Virginia that has need of your services to develop a policy on strip mining."

Madeleine nodded, vaguely thinking about how she would feel going back to the research and the papers. It was where she preferred to be, certainly. Not in the field. Not working directly with the candidate. That part of her life was over.

"Is everything all right, Madeleine?"

"Shouldn't I be asking *you* that?"

"We've already established that I'm terrible. Not much more to be said there. I would rather talk about your woes. Distract me. Please."

Madeleine shook her head. She was being ridiculous. Missing something that wasn't even gone yet. And she certainly wasn't going to discuss her personal feelings with Ben. They were close, but they weren't that close.

She wondered if Ben was that close to anyone.

"I don't have any woes. And I have to catch a flight in a little bit. I wanted to check on you before I left. Anna mentioned the next round of treatment starts soon."

"So it does."

"Good luck."

"Thanks. I'll need it."

Madeleine gave him a brief nod then turned to leave. She stopped when she reached the door. "Please tell me whatever you said to Anna wasn't awful enough to make her leave you. Not now when you need her the most."

"It probably was." He sighed. "But I doubt she'll leave, anyway."

Comforted by that, Madeleine left his office and went in search of Anna. She found her in the kitchen huddled over a cup of tea. When the younger woman looked up, Madeleine could see she'd been crying.

"Don't ask."

"You know, you two have a lot in common."

"He is an ass. And I have nothing in common with an ass."

Madeleine didn't comment. "Is it okay for me to leave with everything going on? I can't let him face what's coming alone, Anna. I owe him that much."

"Don't worry. He won't be alone. I'll be here. Right where I've always been."

But things would be different. Something had obviously happened between them to make everything different. She'd never felt such tension from either of them before.

"You know you can always call me. Talk to me."

Anna nodded, her eyes tearing once more. "Thanks. I appreciate it. I'll keep you up-to-date about his progress. I promise."

Feeling strangely sad, Madeleine did something she wasn't accustomed to doing. She walked over and wrapped her arm around the woman's back and rubbed it until she felt Anna relax. "It's going to be okay. He's going to be okay. I know it," Madeleine said softly.

"Sure. It will all be okay."

"I'll call."

"We'll be here. Just one big happy-ass family. Oh, no, wait…just a boss and his…secretary."

MICHAEL PULLED INTO his assigned parking spot in the garage under his office building and turned off the engine. He'd started the day with an extra burst of excitement since he knew Madeleine would be returning this afternoon. They were to meet at her hotel later and he wasn't foolish enough to convince himself he wasn't counting the hours.

But when he opened his car door he heard someone shout his name.

"Hey, Mickey!"

No, not his name. His old name, his old life, calling out to him in a place where he least expected it. Only Archie and Darnell still called him Mickey. And one other person he didn't want to think had followed him here to his office.

Michael stared at the man who had obviously been waiting for him.

"Good to see you again, Mickey."

Michael closed the car door behind him and the sound of the beep signaling he'd locked the vehicle echoed off the cement walls. "Look, I'm sorry. I know you think we knew each other, but…"

"Come on, don't pull that with me. I know you're playing."

"Not really. I don't play much."

"Okay, I get it," Nooky said, his hands raised as if he was surrendering. "We don't know each other. Never did time together at County. Eighteen years ago. In Block B."

Michael sighed. It was pointless to deny his past, no matter how much he didn't want to go back there. Besides, Archie believed ex-cons needed to stick together. It's how they got a leg up in the world after they got out. Nooky must have told Archie about their meeting and no doubt Archie bragged about Michael. About his success, his job.

Where he worked.

Not that Michael could ever be angry or upset with Archie for giving away such information. He could, however, be slightly annoyed.

"So how is the job going?" Michael asked, trying to stay casual and not leap to conclusions about why Nooky was here.

"The job," Nooky snorted. "Whatever. I never really saw myself as a mechanic. After I got out the first time I stayed clean for a while working at a restaurant. But things got bad and a few jewelry stores later I'm back inside. You know how it goes."

He didn't. One experience had been enough to change everything for Michael. "Yeah, yeah. Listen, I'm late for an appointment…"

"Oh, sure. An appointment. Because you're important, right?"

There was something hard and mean in the man's eyes. With a heavy dose of resentment mixed in. Michael braced himself for what was coming.

"What do you want, Nooky?"

"Look, I'm doing the job. Trying to stay clean and shit. But I was thinking since you're doing so well and Archie says you like to help ex-cons, maybe you could help me out. I mean, we share a common history and everything."

Michael understood paying people off. He'd done it with several people he was concerned might someday be problematic to him. But this straggler was someone who happened to recognize him because he was in the cell next to him. Was it worth it?

"What kind of help do you need?"

"A couple large might do it. Get me back on my feet for real. I mean, look at you. You kept your nose clean all this time and you're a big shot."

Michael didn't become a big shot by simply keeping his nose clean, but he didn't think explaining the concept of ambition to Nooky Clarke was going to make a difference.

"I saw you on the news promoting one of your environmental causes. You're becoming like a real celebrity. Seems to me you like to give your money away. Why not give it to someone you know?"

"Someone I know," Michael repeated. It would be an easy thing to do. Head to the bank, take out some cash and make this reminder of his past go away. Of course, the money would come with the condition that he leave Archie's immediately. After all, Michael deserved at least that much in return for two large.

But something in him balked at the idea. He didn't want to give Nooky the satisfaction that the past bothered Michael so much he was willing to pay to make it go away.

He took a step closer and watched as Nooky shrank back. "Just because you know me, you think that entitles you to a couple thousand dollars of my money? Let me explain something. When you're going to attempt to blackmail someone you really need to have an implied threat. Otherwise there is no motivation on my part to give you what you want. So what is your threat, Nooky? Why should I agree to give you what you want?"

The man held his hands up again and Michael could see the grease he hadn't bothered to clean off. "Hey, nobody said nothing about blackmail. I was looking for a little charity. That's all."

"I save my handouts for the people who need them. You have a job. You're getting paid. You're fine. Now, if we're done...?"

Instantly the man's face changed. Gone was the pretense that this was a friendly conversation between two ex-cons who once did time together. Michael stepped around him and headed for the elevators.

"I don't think we're done yet, Mickey. You want a threat? I'll find a way to come up with a threat."

"Good luck."

Michael kept his back to the man as he hit the button on the elevator. He wasn't concerned about any kind of physical attack from behind. He remembered Nooky well enough to know which side of the line he fell on in terms of weak or strong. He'd been a weasel who'd survived by doing whatever was asked of him, whether it was by the guards or the other inmates.

As he stepped onto the elevator he considered his actions and wondered if maybe he had made a mistake. A couple of thousand dollars and he could have made him disappear. Michael believed in taking the easy road when it came to sticky situations and money typically made things very, very easy.

It was the audacity of the weasel's request. *Hey, you and me once did time and you made it, so now you owe me.* It sickened Michael and made the shame of what he'd been back then resurface. It also made him angry enough to tell Nooky to take a hike.

He could only hope this loose end didn't wind up biting him in the ass.

LATER THAT AFTERNOON AS HE WAS leaving the office, Michael was reminded of what it felt like to actually have his ass bitten. His car had been keyed from hood to rear, both driver's and passenger's sides. Deep, ugly, sickening grooves marred the sleek beauty of the machine he'd rebuilt to satisfy his every whim.

To him, it was like desecrating the Mona Lisa.

Nooky's anger had obviously been underestimated.

Approaching his car, he cursed under his breath and stopped when he saw the scrap of paper tucked under his windshield wiper. He pulled out the note and continued to curse.

Why hadn't he paid the little shit off? Forget thousands, a couple of hundred would have been enough to get him to back off and he had that in his wallet.

You want a threat? How's this? Do all them fancy people know what you did to Ricca?

Seeing the name printed on the paper was enough to nearly make him sick. Michael stood for a few minutes and contemplated his options. He could shout and slam his fist into the side of his car, but that would accomplish nothing and would likely further damage either the car or possibly himself.

The more sensible, rational option was simply to throw the note away. He would dismiss it for now, and if Nooky had the balls to come through with another threat then he would see about taking care of the situation. It was what a grown man did. It was so very different from what the hothead he'd once been would have done. The hothead would already be nursing a hand with broken bones.

In the meantime, he was supposed to be picking up Madeleine at her hotel. He would focus on that. He'd been waiting all day for that.

In the few days she'd been gone her absence had been palpable. He understood why she'd needed to leave. She had work she was still committed to and, of course, she'd wanted to see Ben.

Plus, there wasn't really anything for her to do here. He was sponsoring a marathon on Sunday to promote another green initiative. An event she wouldn't attend. And she was still negotiating with her friend Peg regarding the televised interview, but that could be done from anywhere.

It seemed they were in a waiting game at this point. Letting all the charitable work he'd done sink in with the people who mattered, and until the interview was confirmed there was nothing else he could take on that would instantly remake his image.

Which meant any day now she would announce she was leaving for home permanently.

There was nothing he could do to hold on to her.

Rattled, by the note and her imminent departure, Michael took the long way around town to the hotel. He needed time to get control over his emotions before he saw her, otherwise he might fall to his knees and place his head on her stomach and beg her not to leave him.

That would definitely not be cool. After battling downtown traffic for more than forty minutes, his head was clearer and he felt like he was better able to deal with seeing her. He could be his normal, casual self. An unthreatening friend.

That was what he remained as he knocked and heard her scrambling inside the suite. But when she opened the door the smile on her face was like nothing he'd ever seen before. His heart beat hard and his stomach leaped and he wondered if he wasn't going to disgrace himself by falling to his knees after all.

IT WAS TOO good to see him. Too exciting. Too everything. She shouldn't be this happy.

"Hi," she said and could hear the breathless quality in her voice. She was pathetic. She was a sixteen-year-old waiting for a boy to pick her up for the prom. Not that she knew what that felt like from experience. Her father had frowned on the idea of something as silly as a dance with a boy when she could be studying instead.

Ugh, she didn't want to think about her father now. She needed to have more control over her thoughts than this.

"Hi."

Swinging open the door she let him inside. "You're late."

"Traffic."

Madeleine was at a loss as to what came next. Her skin felt prickly and her tongue felt thick. They were supposed to go over the schedule for the marathon, which was going to include a brief speech from him to kick it off. They had been doing this kind of work for weeks now, but suddenly it all felt strange.

She'd missed him. A couple of days away and she'd missed him. She was a fool to think she could stay away from him indefinitely. Which led her to wonder what the hell she was going to do when it came time to go home. Because she did have to go home eventually. The job wouldn't last forever.

"Do you want to talk about the speech first?" She needed to focus on the work. The work was the barrier between them she couldn't forget.

Michael already had his suit jacket off and was pacing in front of the television. She wondered if he knew how often he did that. Back and forth, back and forth, like he couldn't stop himself. Like one of those office desk toys—once they were set in motion, the motion never ended.

"No, I'm not ready for speech talk. How was your trip?"

"Fine. Good. I was able to finish up a job that had been lingering. And I was able to visit Ben. He's lining up more work for me when I return."

"I don't want to talk about you returning, either. How is Ben?"

Madeleine, who had long since given up the pretense of formality when working with Michael, hadn't even bothered to put her shoes on when she answered the door. Barefoot and wearing the casual slacks she'd flown in, she sat on the small suite couch and tucked her feet up underneath her.

"Not great. The current treatment isn't working as the doctors had hoped. There are stronger chemotherapy drugs they can try, but as weak as he is now, I don't know how much more he can take. Plus, he and Anna seemed to be fighting about something."

"So? You said they were close. His illness is bound to cause stress and tension. Sometimes fighting can relieve that."

"Yes, but this felt different. I've always wondered about their relationship. Yes, she works for him, but there always seemed to be something more. But when I was there visiting it was like that spark was gone. It felt like she was pulling away from him. Certainly not what he needs right now."

Michael sat on the coffee table in front of the couch. He reached out to take her hand. Madeleine let him hold it. She definitely wasn't pulling away. At least not from him.

"I'm sorry."

"Me, too."

"I'll be here for you. If you need me."

Would she need him? If something happened to Ben, would she need to be held and comforted? The answer was yes, as long as it was Michael doing the comforting.

This time she did pull her hand away. She unfurled her legs and stood. It was her turn to pace. She needed to find her shoes. She should find her shoes and put on some lipstick. No doubt her makeup had all worn off. She probably looked worn-out. Vulnerable. She shouldn't have answered the door without those shields in place.

"Are you hungry?" he asked her. "I'm starved."

Dinner, food. Practical things like that helped to keep her focused on something besides him. Because his presence seemed to suck up all the air in the room. Madeleine decided she was famished.

"Yes. I can order up room service. What were you thinking?"

Michael joined her at the desk, where she was thumbing through the room-service menu. A menu they had ordered from so many times already because she wouldn't eat with him anywhere besides Darnell's.

He reached around her to put his hand on the book and close it. "No room service. I'm sick of it. Eat with me downstairs in the restaurant."

"Michael, I don't want to go there again. You know I won't be seen with you," she said quietly, feeling his body heat as he stood inches behind her.

"Fine. Then come to my place. It's private. I can cook for you."

She turned and was sorry she had because he seemed even closer now that she was looking at him. "Michael…"

"Madeleine. We've been down this road. You know I'm not going to pounce on you as soon as I get you in my home. I want to relax, have a nice dinner, maybe some wine. We'll talk about the speech and we'll talk about our working plans for the future."

Her heart was beating as hard as if she'd just run a sprint. "You promise?"

"I promise we're not going to do anything you don't want to do."

Madeleine hated statements like that. It meant if she caved, when she caved, it would be all her fault. Of course, if she did cave then that's exactly what it would be.

Her fault. Her fault for not fighting her feelings harder, for not exerting more control over her mind and her body.

Her fault for being weak. But only when it came to him.

All she had to say was no. All she had to do was send him on his way, let him know she would be in touch with him regarding the interview and call an end to their working arrangement. She could go back to Philadelphia, put him behind her and move on with her life.

Her ruthlessly controlled and freezing-cold life. A life she was coming to believe she had grown tired of. It was in her power to change it.

"Okay." The word was more of a whisper, but she watched him smile slowly.

"Don't look so nervous. I'm a good cook."

She tried to smile, but could feel it wobble. He took her hand and walked her over to the door, where her shoes were waiting for her. She stepped into them without releasing his hold. He continued to grasp her hand as he led her out of the suite and down the elevator to the parking garage and his car.

When she saw the key marks she gasped, but he dismissed it as the work of some juvenile delinquents. Then she stopped thinking about the car altogether.

She was going with him, willingly, to his house. Leaving the safety of her hotel and breaking away from seven years of strictly followed rules. Madeleine tried to tell herself it didn't have to mean anything. She could control her every action. It would be dinner and conversation and nothing else.

She almost believed it.

CHAPTER EIGHT

"MORE WINE?" Michael tilted the bottle at the edge of her glass, waiting for her answer. He could see the hesitation and wanted to tell her she was as safe with him after two glasses of wine as she was after only one. But they'd had a nice dinner and he didn't want to remind her of the tension they had each felt before.

When she'd opened the door of her hotel suite the jolt had been physical. He felt it and he knew she felt it, too. They were two people standing on either side of an entrance, afraid to move because of what might happen if they did.

Michael hadn't felt anything like it since he'd been in high school and in lust for the first time with Carol McGrady.

But he wasn't in high school anymore and nothing that happened between them would be as innocent. They both had too much baggage for that to be the case.

Eventually Madeleine nodded an answer

to his question and he tipped the expensive Chardonnay over until it filled her glass.

"You were right about your cooking. This was delicious."

"I can make two things. Hot dogs and salmon. I figured you would prefer salmon." They had stopped at a local fish place and picked up their dinner. A few vegetables along with flavored instant rice and the meal was simple but satisfying.

He liked having her in his home more than he could say. There were no fancy-restaurant airs. No waiters or waitresses tripping over themselves to be nice once they recognized him. Nobody interrupted their conversation with requests to take their plates away or for water refills.

They simply sat around the island in his kitchen on high stools and ate and talked.

"Your home is lovely," she commented, her eyes looking out at the great room that extended past the kitchen.

He guessed it was. He'd paid handsomely for it to be so. He'd told the decorator that he wanted elegance and sophistication. They were the most opposite things he could think of from his days growing up in the trailer. He wanted pretty where there had been grime.

Expensive things where there had been only trash.

He wished he'd had more connection to the things that had been bought for him. He hadn't thought to pick out the art pieces he liked, or choose between different color schemes. He'd given everything over to the decorator without really thinking about what it meant to create a home.

Sometimes it made him feel like a stranger in his own house, but he couldn't fault the decorator for that.

"Thank you. I hoped it would impress you."

"You think you needed a house to impress me?"

"I knew my faultless manners weren't going to do the trick." He smiled. "You might have noticed I can be a little rough around the edges at times."

"At times. But it's what makes you you. And I'm not impressed by a house."

"No?"

She shook her head. "I am impressed by the man, however. The very smart man who created a very incredible car that I believe will have the effect you want and revolution-ize how we think about driving."

"You're good for my ego. Sure I can't convince you to move to Detroit to be my cheer-leader?"

He watched her face change. She tried to hide it as she took another sip of her wine. Was it disappointment? It certainly was awkward. Not one for subtlety, he pushed the issue.

"Look, I know we're coming up on the end here. There's really not much more you can do to shine me up."

"I think if Peg agrees to the interview, you'll need help with the prep. But you're right, other than that I don't know if you really need me anymore." She set her glass on the granite top and slowly pushed it away from her. Like she would soon push him away.

"That's not true. I do need you," he said abruptly. He got down from his stool and moved toward her. He crossed his arms over his chest and thought about what he could say, what he could ask.

"Michael, don't do this. We both know this wasn't going to be anything more than a temporary work assignment. Yes, I think we've also developed a…friendship. And if I leave on good terms, then we can continue being friends."

"I don't want you to go. Tell me I'm wrong, but I don't think you want to leave."

She got down from the chair and took a few steps away from him, at least out of arm's reach. "Michael, I like you. And yes, I'm probably going to miss our friendship, but if you thought there could be anything else between us, you were wrong. If for no other reason than you're going someplace I can't follow."

"I'm not going anywhere. I'm building a car. I'm partnering up with a large company. That's it. End of story."

"No, you'll see. With your enthusiasm, your passion, you'll be the face of whatever this turns out to be. You'll be huge. People will know you. They'll know everything about you. They'll certainly know who you are dating."

Michael moved toward her, closing the distance. He was a fool to be pushing this, he knew it, but he couldn't stop himself. He needed her. It was the only thought that rang true in his thick, stubborn skull. And she wasn't saying she wasn't interested. She was saying she didn't like the idea of him being famous.

"You're speculating. You have no idea what this is going to turn out to be. Admit you're afraid of the way you feel about me and that's why you're running." She shook her head and it aggravated him like no gesture he'd ever seen before. "You're lying."

Madeleine stopped backing up. "I'm not. And I'm not running away. I'm going home. It isn't out of fear—it's because that's where I belong."

"Like hell it isn't about fear."

"It's about self-preservation. It's about not making the same mistakes I made before. I don't want a man who has anything to do with the media or the press. I can't have cameras in my life. I can't do it."

"Then who do you want? Anybody? Have you felt like this for anybody since your oh-so-tragic fall?"

Nobody had ever said he wasn't ruthless. Not one person, even after he had changed his life so drastically, had told Michael Langdon he was a nice guy. He sure as hell didn't feel nice. He felt a little crazy, like this precious thing was slipping through his fingers and he couldn't find a way to make it stop.

"We're friends. You said that's all you wanted."

"Sorry, sweetheart. I saw the way you smiled at me when you opened that door today. I know better. You want me. I know it. You think I can't see it when you look at me?"

"Shit."

The foul word coming from her Ivy League lips stunned him. He realized he'd put her on this pedestal of femininity and class. To hear her curse, and do so over him, made him feel like laughing and scooping her up in his arms and twirling her about.

"What do you want from me, Michael? Why are you pushing me?"

He couldn't say what he wanted. He only knew what he didn't want. "I don't want you to go. Stay here with me. Let's see what could happen. Don't we owe ourselves that? A chance at maybe…I don't know…happiness?"

She crossed her arms over her chest and raised her head up as if seeking divine intervention. "That's not going to happen. I still work for you. If you think I'm going to set up house here and be your little lady…that's not going to happen."

"You're right. I was stupid. I forgot one last thing."

This time Michael did pounce. He had his hands around her upper arms, holding her in place. He felt like a predator who had latched on to something too big for him to hold, but hold her he did.

"Madeleine, you're fired."

It was the last thing he said before he swooped down and kissed her.

SHE COULD HAVE PUSHED him away. He hadn't used his strength against her, only his desire and his insistence. She could have pushed him away, asked him to take her back to the hotel, never to see him again.

Just like she could have stopped what happened with the president.

This is different.

The thought crept into her mind and she acknowledged the truth of it. This wasn't like the last time. This didn't feel dirty or tawdry. This didn't feel like spinning out of control. Maybe because Michael was nothing like the president. He always listened to her.

The truth was, she wanted this kiss. She'd thought about it for days, maybe even weeks. He'd been right. When she'd opened the door to him earlier that evening she could have put her arms around him and kissed him with everything she had inside of her.

It's what she'd wanted to do. It's what she'd done in her mind. But the controlled, sensible and cold Madeleine prevailed.

Yet when she accepted his invitation for dinner at his house, she intentionally brought herself to this place, knowing the intimacy between them would only grow.

A hotel room was sterile and cold, but this was where he lived. Where he ate and cooked. Watching him with a goofy smile on his face as he mashed up the instant-rice bag before putting it in the microwave had been charming. Teasing him as he tried to carefully turn the fish in the sauté pan without breaking it apart had been fun.

She'd been deluding herself if she'd thought this night was going to end any other way. It was time to be honest with herself about why she'd broken her rules. The only reason was that she wanted this. She wanted him.

She put her arms around his waist. Feeling the muscles in his back clench as she leaned into his kiss was pure joy.

He broke away from her lips and captured her cheeks in his hands. "Madeleine, don't tease me."

"Was I teasing you?"

His lips curled. "No, you were kissing me."

"I like doing that."

"Me, too." He paused as if unsure what came next.

"I'm tired of fighting it, Michael. What-ever this is, it's something, right?"

"It's something," he said, but she could see a distraction about him. He was thinking, planning, looking for the place they had to go next. She didn't want him to do that. She didn't want to think too much about any-thing.

"Kiss me again," she demanded.

Gently he cradled her face in his hands and brought his lips to hers. "Madeleine," he moaned. "You're killing me."

She felt a tension in him she didn't quite understand. There was no ease in his kiss. No melting sense of rightness now that they had finally given in to what they both wanted. He was kissing her with purpose, but she didn't sense he was letting himself become aroused like he was arousing her.

She moved her body against him and felt him back his hips away.

"It's okay. I give up. I surrender."

He looked at her then, trying to understand what she was saying. "What are you saying...?"

"Michael, make love to me. That's what I'm saying."

He let her go then and took a cautious step back. Again, not something she was expecting.

"Isn't that what you wanted?" Doubt started

to creep in. Maybe he wasn't sure what he wanted.

"I want you," he said roughly. "I want you like you can't understand. What I feel inside, it's like this thing trying to bust out of me."

Yet she could still sense his hesitation. She took a step toward him this time. "Then take me upstairs. I've been in ice for seven years and I want to get warm. I want to feel heat. Make me warm. Please."

He grabbed her hands and bent his head, kissing her on the knuckles. "You sure about this?"

"Yes. You were right about everything. I was going to run because I was afraid. But suddenly I don't feel afraid anymore."

"Okay. Okay. We can do this."

He took her hand and she nearly had to jog to keep up with him. She was about to tell him she didn't believe this was a race to anything but he was leading her up the stairs and all words fell away. Two French doors opened into the master bedroom, which was decorated with chocolate-brown tones and dark purple accents.

He turned to her again and kissed her. Again she felt a tension she didn't understand. She couldn't tell if he was rushing because he was desperate to make love to her or because he wanted to get it over with.

"Michael, stop." Madeleine pushed away from him, feeling as if she was some sort of goal he wanted to reach. Rather than feeling like a woman who was about to become his lover.

He backed off and his eyes never left her lips. "What?"

"Are you sure you want this? We don't have to…"

"No. Of course we have to. I have to." He shook his head. "I want to. Let me…" His voice trailed off and he left her standing in the middle of the room while he walked away from her.

"I'm going to change real quick."

She watched him walk toward another door that she imagined led to a closet, but when he turned the light on she could see it was a tiled bathroom. Maybe he kept a robe on the door? He swung the door nearly closed, and she couldn't help but wonder what was making him so nervous.

It wasn't helping the situation. She was already anxious enough for both of them. It would have been so much easier to simply rely on him to take the lead and make things calm for her. But it didn't seem like that was going to happen and it confused her.

The man was a known playboy, so it wasn't as if having a woman in his bedroom was new to him. Or maybe it was. Maybe he didn't bring those women back to this place. Maybe he was nervous because what was about to happen between them was special.

At least, that's what she wanted. She wanted it to be very special.

Looking around, she took in the room. She expected his bedroom to be more personal than downstairs. Maybe pictures of his racing wins or of Archie. But there was nothing. Impersonal art decorated the walls and elegant pillows were sprawled on the bed. The floor underneath her feet was hardwood covered in thick lush rugs that would make it bearable walking from the bed to the bathroom on a cold winter night.

She could hear him moving about in the bathroom. He'd been in there for a couple of minutes. He was taking nervous to a whole other level. It looked like it was going to be up to her to calm them both.

"Michael, you know you don't have to be worried."

There was a pause, then "Huh?"

"I mean this is supposed to be fun. Yes,

maybe this is going somewhere between us, but I don't want to put a lot of pressure on us for some earth-shattering experience. Let's just relax and take it easy. We have all night, don't we?"

"All night," he echoed. Then she thought she heard him curse under his breath. Suddenly the sound of little objects tapping along the bathroom floor could be heard. She watched as something slid out under the door and rolled along the hardwood floor in her direction.

Walking over, she bent down and picked up what turned out to be a little blue pill. The drug's name was printed in neat, tiny letters. She read it and stunning disbelief slammed into her. Followed quickly by the thought that he wouldn't do this to her. That he *couldn't* be doing this to her. Not him. But the evidence was in her hand.

"Don't," he said as he pushed open the bathroom door. He was dressed in a silk robe. "Give me that!"

She pulled her hand away even as he reached for it. "This? You need this to sleep with me?"

His eyes closed and he seemed to be mumbling, or possibly praying. When he opened them he looked at her and said very slowly, "Madeleine, you need to listen to me."

But she couldn't hear anything beyond the buzzing in her ears. He was known for chasing women all over the world. Actresses, supermodels, car groupies. He'd never been seen without a woman draped all over him in a picture and yet for her, he required prescription stimulation.

"Is this some kind of sick...?" She couldn't finish. She couldn't imagine what this was. But she knew at least one thing. He didn't want her. He wasn't aroused by her. He simply wanted to have sex with her. Like those other men did, like she was some kind of prize to be won. A novelty to be used and discarded.

She flung the pill at him.

"Madeleine, wait."

Why, when there was no point? She knew who he was now and she didn't want to listen to any excuses he might offer. It would only hurt more if he tried to justify his actions. She turned and started running for the stairs, but he reached out to grab her arm.

"Let go of me," she snapped, feeling the anger rise through her body. "You don't want me. This was all some kind of elaborate ploy on your end. What did you think, Michael?

Did you think banging the woman who banged the president would somehow make you more appealing to those car executives?"

"Stop it."

"Stop what? Stop saying the truth? That I don't interest you? That you need a pill to be with me? Why would you do this to me when you knew…?" Her voice cracked. "I told you about those other men. What they wanted from me, what they thought they were entitled to. How could you?"

She wrenched her arm away from him and started down the stairs. She needed to get to her purse, and then get out of the house. She could call a cab company from down the block.

"Madeleine, don't do this! Please!"

She wasn't going to listen to him. Nothing he said would be true. All of it would be an excuse. She was so sick of excuses. When was she going to learn? She couldn't trust anyone.

He was following her and she didn't slow down. She'd left her purse on a bench in the foyer. If she could reach that, then the door…

"Madeleine!"

She'd never know what stopped her. Maybe it was the sound of desperation she heard in his voice. She turned and he was behind her crouched down on his haunches, his hands covering his face. His fingers running through his hair and gripping it as if he meant to tear it out.

"Ahhh!" He barked out a curse and in it she heard not an excuse, not some easy explanation, but a man in real anguish.

Oh, no.

Slowly, cautiously, as if she was approaching a feral animal, she made her way back to him. He must have heard the sound of her shoes on the floor because he eventually lifted his head. His eyes were red with unshed tears.

She gulped, feeling now that she had committed some horrible crime against this man. "Tell me," she said softly.

"I don't need the pill because I don't want you. I want you. I want you so much. I need the pill because…because…"

She watched him try to work the words out as if they were too difficult to say. She stepped closer, giving him the courage he needed.

"Because I can't without it."

She nodded and let out her breath. "Since when?" she asked, thinking of all the women in all the pictures over the years. Had there been an accident recently? Maybe during his last car race? All sorts of scenarios flittered through her mind.

He shook his head as if knowing what she was guessing at, as if to say none of what she thought was true.

Then he laughed. A terrible and awful laugh. "You want the truth?"

"Of course I do."

"The truth is I haven't been able to get it up without medication since I was nineteen years old. The day after Ricca Valente raped me in prison."

And that was the one scenario she hadn't considered.

CHAPTER NINE

MICHAEL STRAIGHTENED AND started walking back to the stairs with some idea that he would climb them and never look back and that the staircase would go on forever. But when he got to the bottom, he decided he didn't have the energy to make the climb. So he sat on the step and waited for the sound of the front door closing.

Only it never came. *Damn.* He might have been able to live with her disgust. What had happened to him was disgusting. What he couldn't live with, what he didn't want, was her pity.

She came to him, walking gingerly as if a sudden motion might shatter him.

"Go away, Madeleine. Just go away."

"I don't think that's going to happen."

"It's over. This is over between us. You wouldn't let me pretend so now we can have nothing."

"You're right about one thing. I won't let you pretend. I'll never let you pretend with me. But this thing between us is a long way from over." She sat on the stairs next to him, not touching him. Not saying anything for a while.

"I'm sorry I accused you of being one of those men who would use me. That was my past talking."

"Fine," he said dully. "Leave."

He felt like he had a hundred pillows stuffed inside his head. Why had he said it? Why had he told her the truth? In eighteen years he'd never told anyone the truth but the shrinks who had tried to treat him. Not even Archie. Certainly never a woman.

It had to be her? The one person who made him feel close to being a man again and he'd blurted out his greatest mortification.

"We're going to talk about this, Michael."

The hell they were. "There is nothing to talk about. I want you to go. I can call you a cab. Pack your things and head back to Philadelphia."

"I don't think so."

He looked at her then, but quickly looked away because he couldn't stand to see the sincerity in her expression. Sincerity was pity's twin sister and neither was appealing to him. Her voice had this authoritative tone, which she used when she felt she was really right about something. It made him realize why she had risen through the political ranks so quickly. When she said something in that tone, you had no choice but to listen.

Only not this time. He wasn't going to talk about it and he needed a way to get her to leave. He needed a hot shower, a bottle of booze and at least twenty-four hours before he would be able to live in his skin again and not feel the shame oozing from each pore.

"What do you want to talk about, Madeleine? The details? You want me to walk you through it, break it down…"

She put her hand on his arm and squeezed. "Stop it. You know I don't want to make you relive that. I only want to know why…"

"Why I didn't tell you when we first met?" he asked, feeling the sarcasm build inside. "Hello, my name is Michael Langdon and I'm the victim of a sexual assault. Yes, folks, all those horrible tales you hear about prison are, in fact, true. You've got to watch your back in the shower…"

He didn't see the hand that had been holding his arm lift, but he sure felt the slap across his cheek. A pretty good one, too. So hard he was momentarily startled.

"I'm sorry," she said, shaking a little. "I

don't know why I did that. I've never struck anyone in my life."

Michael couldn't say the same. Maybe deep down there was a little violence in Madeleine.

"Don't talk to me like that. Like I'm some nobody in your life. Like I'm someone who doesn't care." She shifted to look him in the eye so he could see she was legitimately angry.

"I don't know what you want from me. I have nothing to give. Not answers. Not anything."

"Nothing? So you're impotent…"

He winced at the word. Always did.

"And that's it. To you, everything else doesn't matter. What we felt for each other. All that talk about maybe having a chance at happiness… What was all that? Bullshit?"

Yes, she was firing mad and he could still feel the sting on his cheek. If he wasn't so dead inside he might have thought it was arousing. Madeleine was always beautiful to him, but on fire like this, she was electric.

"No. Yes. No, it wasn't bull, but we certainly don't have any chance now. You know. You know what I am."

"Michael, other than the fact that you have

a condition brought on by trauma, there's not a whole lot I see different about you."

A condition brought on by trauma. It's what all his shrinks said. And none of them had been able to fix him. There had been a moment, though, at the hotel-room door, when he'd thought he might be cured. His body knew what it wanted, even if his head wouldn't let him forget.

For the first time in eighteen years Madeleine had nearly brought him to the brink of salvation with a smile. But when he'd stood in his bathroom looking at himself in the mirror, knowing he didn't deserve her, the thought of Nooky and what he'd written on his note came back to him. As the memories descended, any hope of being with Madeleine, really being with her, was gone. Any desire he'd felt turned into self-disgust.

He'd cursed and reached for the pills and popped off the damn top and spilled them everywhere. Why had he done that? When he'd always been so careful to hide it before?

"I want another glass of wine."

She left him there on the steps. He heard her fussing about in his kitchen, getting another glass and pulling out the bottle from the refrigerator. She wasn't going to leave. That much was obvious. Getting up, he followed her and found some whiskey in his liquor cabinet.

Madeleine moved around his home differently. Where before she had been cautious and almost skittish, now she seemed comfortable and more in control. He couldn't say he blamed her.

"You're not worried I'm going to pounce on you anymore, are you?"

She took a sip of her drink. "I was never worried you were going to pounce. I was worried I was going to cave. Which, of course, I did. I wanted you very much."

"Don't try to placate me, Madeleine. I'm not some toothless lion to be led around by the paw."

She smiled grimly at that. "No, you're not toothless."

He poured a generous amount of whiskey over ice and then joined her in the living room, where she sat on the couch.

"Does that fireplace work?"

Michael found the remote control and turned the gas on. He wasn't sure what was happening. He was about to sit in the leather chair across from the couch when she patted the open spot next to her.

For a moment he thought about ordering her out of his home. If he yelled really loudly, scared her with the heat of the temper he knew lingered inside him, he might be able to force her to leave.

As if reading his thoughts, she said, "I'm not going anywhere. No matter what you say. I can see it in your eyes. You're standing there looking at me like I'm three-day-old leftovers you don't want to eat. Well, tough. I'm here and I'm not going anywhere."

Michael shrugged and sat next to her on the couch. She leaned into him, relaxing her weight on him so he was forced to hold her. Her back was against his chest. He took a deep gulp of the brown liquor and felt the heat of it sliding down his throat. It reminded him he wasn't completely numb.

"Those women you were with…did any of them know?"

The questions he expected. Of course she would want to know things, pick apart his actions, figure him out. He decided there were things he would answer and things he wouldn't.

"No. I was always very careful. There is nothing physically wrong with me and the little blue pill works when I need it. You should also know that I was tested. For everything. And with those other women I always wore a condom. I need you to know I would never put you in any kind of risk that way."

"Yes, I know that. Do you… I mean, can you… Is it pleasurable for you?"

Even with everything that had happened, he still found his lips curling. Poor modest little Madeleine. Such a hard topic for her. How anyone who knew her could have thought she was some promiscuous home wrecker was inconceivable.

"Do I come?"

"I guess that's a way of putting it."

"No. I never get there. I make sure they have a good time and they never know the difference."

"Yes, but it's why you were never with the same woman twice. Always someone new so they would never suspect after being with you for a prolonged time."

He shrugged. While that was the reality of his life, it wasn't always about hiding his condition. He hadn't had any intention of ever getting married, so there was no reason to engage in a serious relationship.

He had fun with them. He partied with them and danced with them and drank with them. He let them adore him, which was always an ego boost. When it came time to perform he made sure they always left completely satisfied.

"Have you seen a psychologist?"

"Yes."

She took a breath then and he knew the next question would be a difficult one. "One of the blips that stands out about your past is the fact that you served the full three years of your sentence. I didn't dig because it didn't seem necessary for what you were trying to do, but I would have thought as a first-time offender you would have been out in less than a year with good behavior."

Michael took another gulp of his drink. He'd told her what he thought was the worst thing about him, but maybe this next truth would be even more disgusting in her mind. She was a woman who believed very much in the system, after all. If it was the final cut to the tenuous string holding them together, so be it.

"I wasn't well behaved. After…it…happened, I was changed. Something inside me was broken and I thought I wasn't ever going to get myself back. You have to understand, in prison it's all about dominance and submission and holding on to your power. Gangs come together to protect one another as much as they do to target the weak. I'd been made a victim. I had only one choice to change that. I found the man who did it in the rec room and whaled on him with every ounce of strength I had. All my anger and my rage… I slammed into his body until finally I beat him into a coma."

"Michael," she whispered.

"No, you need to hear this. You need to know what's inside me. I wanted to kill him. My plan was to kill him. I would not have stopped until he was dead if the guards hadn't pulled me off him. Do you understand? Do you know what it makes me?"

She didn't turn around, but she didn't remove her weight, either. "Yes."

"Do you want to leave now?"

This time she did turn to face him. "Did you think I would go?"

"Yes."

"Well, I'm not. You were in a violent place. You reacted violently. I'm not going to judge that man."

"Well, if you won't, I will." He pushed against her to let her know he wanted up and she obliged. He walked back to his liquor cabinet and poured another drink, then he walked over to the phone in his kitchen.

"What are you doing?"

"Calling a cab."

"I told you I'm not leaving," she said stubbornly.

"Well, you're not staying." He used information to get the number of a cab service and then had them dial the number. He rattled off his address to the dispatcher and was told a car would be by in less than twenty minutes.

She was standing when he came back to the great room. Her arms straight at her sides like she was readying herself for the next attack.

"I want you to leave. Look, not forever… okay. But for tonight. I need…some space."

"Why do I have the feeling if I walk out that door I'll never see you again?"

Because there was a chance it was true. He didn't know what was going to happen next. Not with him, not between them. He did know he needed some time.

"Please," he said.

Finally she nodded. "Okay. I'll go for now. But this isn't over between us. I won't let it be."

He watched her gather her coat and purse and after a few minutes a horn sounded letting them know the cab was there. She didn't say goodbye. He didn't, either, for that matter, but before she left she looked at him and he could see a determination in her face that made him a believer.

No, this definitely wasn't over between them.

CHAPTER TEN

SHE'D COME. Two days of the silent treatment had apparently been enough for her.

He should have been elated. This was the first time she'd ever ventured out into what would be considered a public event. And she'd done it for him. But it was probably only because she was furious with him.

"Okay, everyone, go out there and have a great day. Let the race begin!"

Michael snipped the scissors that sent the tightly strung green ribbon flying. Instantly runners flew through the opening, with the professional marathoners starting at a blistering pace while the first-timers took things slow.

While he didn't envy any of the participants—he would much rather race in a car than on foot—it was a perfect day for the event. Spring was in full bloom and the slight nip of the early morning air would keep the runners from getting overheated.

The race started in Chene Park and would

run along the river for miles until eventually it finished on the other side of the park where the amphitheater was. Some of the bigger contributors were invited to a concert later that evening that would feature some of Detroit's most successful musicians.

For now, Michael concentrated on ignoring the woman tucked off to the side and instead spent time shaking the hands of the other sponsors and event coordinators. While the volunteers broke down the tables and got ready to set up a new camp at the finish line, Michael had his picture taken with people and signed autographs. Basically doing anything he could think of to avoid her.

It wasn't until most everyone was gone but for a few stragglers that he realized he was going to have to talk to her.

She wore sunglasses that nearly covered her face and a ball cap that dipped low over her forehead. To anyone else she was unrecognizable. To him she stood out like a sore thumb.

But she'd come. For him.

It was easy enough for her to know where he was going to be since she was the one who scheduled the event. But it was hard to believe that she had risked coming somewhere

where there were a lot of cameras and even local-TV news crews.

It could only mean she was feeling desperate.

Since he'd put her in a cab and sent her back to her hotel after what he thought of as the "big confession," he hadn't called her or returned any of her messages. It seemed easier to avoid her. Because wanting her, but not being able to have her, being with her, but not being able to make love to her—that seemed like a sure form of torture.

The only thing worse was being separated from her. It was a lose-lose situation for him.

He could tell she was pissed by the way she held her arms crossed over her chest and kept her pointy chin raised in the air. He was going to pay for avoiding her. Probably deservedly so, but it wasn't like he'd planned on sneaking off and never talking to her again. He wasn't a coward or a person who couldn't handle confrontation.

It was just that he was still…thinking.

It was an adjustment to deal with the idea that someone else in the world, someone not paid to keep the secret, knew his darkest nightmare. It was unsettling. That alone made it difficult to be around her. There had to be some allowances given for that. A window of time granted to him to let everything that had happened settle in his mind and his gut. Because he knew when they did talk, she was going to ask more questions about what their relationship might be that he didn't have the answers for.

She would probably still want to try them, to try to make something between them work. Whatever the hell that meant. In his mind, it was a ridiculous notion if sex wasn't going to be included. But even knowing there was no pleasure in it for him, she wouldn't let him take the necessary medication to make sex possible.

A stalemate.

So what was the point?

A platonic relationship?

He supposed it wasn't a bad offer for a man like him. In fact, he remembered thinking when he first met her how perfect Madeleine was for him. She would absolutely not cross the line again and have sex with her employer. So as long as she worked for him he was safe from any type of sexual pursuit from her and of course she was safe from any moves from him. But then everything changed. Because even though he knew he couldn't perform the act, his whole being wanted her like no other woman he'd ever known.

And she'd wanted him the same way. Otherwise she never would have come to his house.

Yes, he might have considered it a great thing that they could take sex completely off the table. Only it didn't feel right with him. There was urgency to the way he felt about her. An intensity that made him feel like a caged animal any time he thought about her. Those feelings didn't go with something that was platonic. It would be like a starving man at a feast where the food was under glass. He could see it, but he couldn't eat it.

So he had spent the past few days thinking. And thinking. Knowing the best thing he could do was to send her back to Philadelphia and out of his life for good. Only he was too selfish to end it that cleanly. He needed to know she was still in Detroit. And now, the way his body tingled at the sight of her in those ridiculous oversize sunglasses, he knew he wasn't any closer to sending her back. He wasn't that strong.

As hard as it was going to be to give her what she wanted, it would be that much harder to cut her out of his life. Her very presence was reeling him in like a fish on a line. He felt so compelled to get closer to her he finally stopped avoiding her and approached.

"What? No burka?"

"I thought it might be overkill."

"This is definitely a first. Aren't you afraid someone might see us?"

"You didn't really give me a choice," she said tightly. "You won't return my calls."

He reached out as if he was going to touch her cheek. Her skin was so perfect, so soft, it was almost like she wasn't real, but she was. He dropped his hand without touching her. She wouldn't like it, anyway. Not in public.

"I needed to think," he said honestly.

"Okay, what have you concluded?"

He raised his eyebrows at that. "You think after two days I've *concluded* anything?"

"Here is what I'm thinking. I'm living out of a suitcase in a very nice suite you're paying for. If you're going to take an indefinite amount of time to *think*, it only makes sense for me to go home."

It made total sense for her to go home. "Don't leave. Not yet."

"You fired me. Remember?"

"So I could be with you."

"Only you've been nowhere near me for two days." Her chin really couldn't get any higher. "You told me that wasn't going to happen. You told me you were only making me leave temporarily otherwise I wouldn't have gone."

"Madeleine, you have to know what this is doing to me."

"Michael, you have to know what this is doing to *me*. You want time, okay. You don't want me to leave Detroit, okay. But you need to talk to me. We're never going to get anywhere if you shut me out."

"I wasn't shutting you out…I was…putting you on hold." He winced as the words came out, knowing how awful they sounded.

She whipped off her sunglasses and pinned him down with a harsh stare. "I'm no one to be put on hold. I have a life. I have friends who need me. What about Ben?"

"What about Ben?" He could feel the anger in his chest building. He didn't like to be pushed or cornered. And he certainly didn't like the idea of her running back to Ben. Sick or not, the man was a force of nature. If Ben ever decided he wanted Madeleine and could give her everything she deserved as a woman, there would be nothing Michael could do to fight it.

"This isn't about Ben. I need to know if your plan is to leave me in that damn suite indefinitely while you continue to *think* and ignore my calls. If so, then what is the point of me staying?"

So he would know she was close. So he would know where to find her when he did want to see her, when he was ready. He didn't imagine she would like those answers, either. Hell, neither did he. He was being irrational and he knew it, but he couldn't wrap his mind around where this was going.

"What do you want from me, then?" he asked. Maybe it would be simpler to figure out what she expected from him.

That stopped her. She opened her mouth, then closed it as if it hadn't even occurred to her what she might want.

"To be with you," she said as if struggling to come up with something that made sense for them. "I guess a date."

"A date? You won't be seen with me in public. Or at least not in public without a disguise."

"We would be safe at the movies."

The movies. It sounded so freaking innocent. A perfectly platonic thing for two people who enjoyed each other's company to do.

He wanted to howl like a monster who was being declawed and defanged.

But in the end he knew she was right. If

he wouldn't talk to her and wouldn't see her then she wouldn't stay.

"Okay. I've got the concert tonight. I don't suppose you would consider…"

"No," she said abruptly. "Too many people and the TV crews will probably come back. They'll want a small clip from you, too. You should have something prepared."

"Yeah, yeah. Okay, movies it is. I'll pick you up tomorrow around six."

Suddenly a flash of something caught his eye. Someone a couple of yards off, who looked like he might be part of the crowd, was paying far too much attention to them. The man wore an oversize hoodie, with the hood draped over most of his face, but the glance he got was enough for Michael to know who it was.

"I like thrillers. And classics. And romantic comedies. Also, I'm going to want peanut M&M's. I can't see a movie without peanut M&M's."

"Got it, M&M's," Michael said without listening. His focus was entirely on the hooded man and what in the hell he was doing at the park.

Then Madeleine moved toward him, like she was about to lean in. Like she was expecting him to drop a simple kiss on her lips, which might be normal for a couple who were dating. But they weren't normal and he wasn't kissing her with the company who was watching them. He stepped back a few steps out of her reach.

"See you then. I've got to run. Set up for the finish and stuff."

"Oh. Right. Okay, then, tomorrow."

"Tomorrow."

He turned his back and walked away, pretending to head to the other end of the event, where the finish line would be set up for runners to start crossing in a couple of hours. After a few minutes, he casually turned around and saw she had left and was headed back to the street, probably to catch a cab.

Not his smoothest move to dismiss her so quickly, but he had business he needed to take care of that he didn't want Madeleine anywhere near. Circling back and using the various groups of people milling about as cover, Michael spotted his target walking around. He moved in quickly until he was a few feet behind the man.

"Looking for me, Nooky?"

The smaller man startled, then rolled his shoulders as if gathering courage before turning around for the confrontation.

"Hey, Mickey, funny we both should be in the park today."

"Not funny at all. Everyone who watched the local news knew I would be here today supporting the marathon."

"You caught me. All your good charitable works, huh. You're like a regular angel now. Not like it was back inside. Back then you were a real mean dude. Real mean. And violent."

Violent, yes. It was how he had felt every day. Violent and nearly desperate to get out. Once free, it was as if he could run away and leave what had happened behind him. Outdistance it. Michael suspected it was one of the reasons that made him such a fast driver.

"Nooky, make your point."

"I think I already made my point with my note. I think you wouldn't like it if all these nice people found out what you really are. I think that should be worth some money to you."

"So you came here today to shake me down?"

"Look, why you gotta make this difficult? A couple large and I'm out of your life for good."

It was tempting. He'd paid off the doctor who'd treated him in the infirmary. He'd even planned to pay off Ricca. If it had taken all his money to erase what had happened, he would have gladly given it. Fortunately, the second payoff wasn't required. After serving five years of his ten-year sentence, Ricca returned home to his gang and was dead from a drive-by within only weeks of being freed.

Michael had learned of Ricca's death when he'd gone looking for him. He'd thought it might have changed something. It hadn't. He knew then that what was broken inside him could never be fixed.

Which was what made the idea of any kind of *relationship* with Madeleine ridiculous. He thought about what she might say if she could see him now. Paying off his past. Trying to use his money to separate himself from the stink. She wouldn't approve. She would want him to do the right thing. The legal thing.

The idea of Madeleine anywhere near this creature made him nauseous. Yet this garbage was part of him. And there wasn't going to be any part of the law in this transaction.

He was about to nod and give his consent to the payoff. Not because the threat meant anything to him. Hell, if he ended up doing the interview it would all come out, anyway. And most CEOs he knew would consider his actions badass.

No, he was doing this to make a problem go away. Plain and simple. Still, something inside him again rejected handing over the money.

Sure, it was the price of doing business. His logical mind knew that. Hell, he should be happy he was getting let off the hook for a couple of thousand. Only he couldn't make himself say the words. His nonlogical brain didn't want to have to pay off this weasel.

Really, what he wanted was *not* to be ashamed.

A word surfaced loud and clear. "No."

"What?"

It rang out in his head. So loud he had to say it again. "No."

"You kiddin' me? I will tell the whole effin' world about you. You got lucky you didn't kill that guy. That's all that separated you from serious time. Face it, you're an animal just like me. And dressing up and cutting ribbons ain't going to change that."

No, it wasn't. But paying off Nooky to go away wasn't going to make what happened go away. Michael knew that now. All the money in the world would never be enough. He'd been kidding himself all this time to think he could buy silence. It seemed there was always going to be another Nooky.

"Nooky, you're right. I haven't changed all that much. The person capable of beating a man to a pulp still lives inside me. So hear this, you're going to go to Archie and quit. You're going to tell your parole officer you need to find another job. You're going to stay away from me for the rest of my life. You see me walking down the street you will turn and walk the other way. You see my face on TV, you'll turn the channel. And you will keep your mouth shut. All knowledge you think you have will disappear from your memory."

"And why am I going to do that?"

"Because if you don't I will hire a private investigator. That investigator will tail you every hour of every day. He will photograph your every move, night and day, for as long as it takes for you to make one mistake which will land you back in jail after your parole is revoked. How many strikes would that be for you, Nooky? I think by my count we're at three. One mistake. You so much as jaywalk and your parole officer will know about it."

"You are damaged, man."

"No, I'm rich. I have all the money in the world to see to it that someone is there when you screw up. How long do you think it will take? How long until you find yourself in need of a piece to protect yourself? Or maybe it will be some illegal substance you'll need so you can sleep at night. Or a girl you'll need to buy because you're too ugly to get one any other way. And that's not even taking into account your need to steal things. Because you like stealing, don't you, Nooky? A stick of gum and you're mine."

Michael could see the beads of sweat forming on Nooky's upper lip. He knew too well he didn't have it in him to go totally straight. He was a lifer, just out for a break.

"Funny thing is, Nooky, I bet I end up paying the investigator less than what you wanted. That's how confident I am you can't stay straight for as long as it takes to tie your shoes. Get out of my face. I see you one more time, my next call is to a P.I."

"This is messed up, man. I just wanted…"

"I don't care what you want. You're not part of my life anymore. Take off. Now!"

With that last shout, Nooky turned and scrambled away. Michael watched him until he was out of sight and wondered if he'd done enough to scare him away indefinitely. Maybe. Maybe not. Either way, it felt good to make a stand and not just against Nooky.

His past was always going to be there. He sure as hell didn't want to linger in it, or even embrace it for that matter, but he was tired of trying to run from something that was strapped to his back like a sack. He had to accept it was there for good and simply carry the load.

It was crazy to think it, but he had a hunch Madeleine would have been proud of him. It gave him a good feeling throughout the rest of the day.

"LADY, can we go? The meter is running."

Madeleine sat in the back of the cab. When she saw Michael confront the man in the park she'd asked the cabdriver to hold up.

"Yes, I'm sorry. We can leave now."

Leaning back against the seat as the cab pulled away, she considered who the man in the hooded jacket might be. She'd spotted him herself and for half a heartbeat feared the paparazzi had seen through her oversize glasses and hat and was about to start snapping pictures. But the man seemed to loiter about with no real intention so she ignored him.

Until Michael all but sprinted away from her. She couldn't say what made her stay and watch the interaction between the two men. Maybe it was the disparity between them. Michael looked sophisticated in beige slacks and a light brown sweater, where the other man looked dirty even from a distance.

She could feel Michael's threatening pose and knew this was no ordinary conversation. The way he towered over the smaller man, it was plain to see his target became increasingly agitated until ultimately he walked away.

Definitely not a fan looking for an autograph.

So who was he? More importantly, would Michael tell her?

Her first thought was that she shouldn't push him if he didn't. She'd succeeded in her goal of getting him to talk to her. That should be enough.

After two days of not hearing from him, she knew his first instinct was to run. Run from her, run from them as a couple. She couldn't let that happen. At least not without a fight.

There was something about him that made her feel different when she was around him. Something she hadn't had...maybe in her whole life. Whatever it was, it felt a lot like need. She wasn't exactly proud to admit that to herself. Madeleine Kane wasn't a woman who *needed* a man. Madeleine Kane was a kingmaker.

Only with Michael she was different. With Michael she was just a woman. A woman he made feel cherished. And despite his impotency...wanted. Very much wanted. For that reason alone it was worth sticking it out and giving everything she had.

She couldn't say where this would end. If she was right and his amazing car did make him bigger than life, she didn't know how long she could hold him offstage with her in the shadows. Because once he walked onstage, she wouldn't follow him.

It was possible she could be setting them both up for a horrible fall. However, it was a risk she was willing to take. And if she was going to convince him that she was equally worth the risk, this was going to have to be more than a date.

Real intimacy was something that came about over time. Madeleine needed to create ties and binds that he wouldn't find easy to shake loose. She was going to have to know everything about him with nothing held back.

She figured he'd given her one secret, the most important of his life. Now it was time to find out all the others.

CHAPTER ELEVEN

"SO ARE YOU going to tell me who that man was with you in the park yesterday?"

Michael turned to her in the darkened theater. He was already halfway through a bag of popcorn and Madeleine was picking out a single peanut M&M at a time to eat when she sprang the question on him.

They had compromised on the movie choice—a re-showing of an old classic. Only two other people were seated on the opposite side of the theater. He could tell it made Madeleine feel more comfortable, almost like having their own private theater. And the other two ticket holders were so far away he knew they wouldn't be able to overhear their whispered conversation.

Not that Michael had any intention of talking to Madeleine about Nooky. There was no point.

"Someone I knew once. He doesn't matter."

"You seemed pretty upset with him."

"You were spying on me?"

"No. Only…watching."

"Why?"

She squirmed in her seat a bit and Michael found himself smiling. He would never tire of unsettling the seemingly unflappable Madeleine Kane.

"I don't know. I thought you were acting strangely. When I leaned in I was hoping you would kiss me. Instead you practically sprinted off. I guess I was lingering for a time while thinking about what that meant. Then I saw you approach the man in the hooded sweatshirt from behind. You looked angry with him."

Michael didn't want to believe there was any sprinting involved. However, he would definitely cop to the fact that he didn't want to be seen kissing Madeleine. Not by Nooky.

"I can't get you to be seen with me in broad daylight, but you thought kissing me in the park was okay."

Madeleine huffed a bit. "First, I was disguised. And second, stop making me out like I'm some kind of vampire. I merely avoid any place where we might be seen together, or could possibly have our picture taken together."

He chuckled at her haughtiness. "True.

You were disguised. And I suppose we did sit outside that day at Darnell's and the sun was out, so we'll have to rule out the vampire thing. But the truth is I don't know how I feel about kissing you. Publicly or otherwise, okay."

She looked at him then, the peanut M&M's forgotten.

"What do you mean?"

He sighed. He supposed if they were going to do this thing, then he had to be completely up front with her. "I want to see you. I want to spend time with you. That's a given."

"But you don't want to kiss me."

"Kissing leads to other things. To places I can't go. I don't know if I want to put myself through that."

He could see her scowl as the light from the movie reflected off her face.

"You're mad," he said. Not exactly the emotion he expected. He was sort of counting on compassion and understanding and hoping that didn't come with a side order of pity. Or worse, disappointment in him.

"You're damn right I'm mad. You're such a man."

"What the hell is that supposed to mean?"

"Why can't kissing just be for the sake of kissing? Why does it have to go anywhere?

You were probably one of those boys in high school who kept track of his game. First base leads to second base, then third base…"

"I get your point." Maybe he had been one of those boys who liked to take things as far as they could go every time, but what horny teenager didn't?

"It's one of the reasons people always saw me as so chaste and pure. One more reason why my downfall was that much more spectacular to those who knew me. I never did the things other girls did in high school."

"Uh, I hope not. You told me you went to an all-girls' school. Although wait…that might be hot."

She elbowed him in the ribs. "There were public schools and an all-boys' Catholic school in the general vicinity for girls who wanted to date."

"But you weren't one of those girls."

"I didn't date much, but there were a few dates. I never cared for the feeling that I was something to be conquered. I liked kissing, but when I was with a boy I always felt like he was lying in wait, ready to pounce and move on to the next step."

"That's because he was. He was a boy."

"And you're a man."

"Have to tell you, we don't change much in that regard."

"My point is we should have grown up, evolved. We can sit here in this theater holding hands and enjoy it. You can take me home and we can make out in the car and enjoy that. Why does it always have to be about what's next?"

Michael considered that and thought only, *because it does*. It was the way of things between men and women who wanted each other. But he knew he didn't like the kid who planted the idea in her head that she was nothing more than a base to steal. He thought it before and he was seeing it again: he wasn't the only one of them in this relationship who was messed up about sex.

It felt to him like Madeleine didn't know what it meant to be wanted for who she was alone, she didn't know what it meant to want that person back for the same reason. He wondered if she'd ever been made love to or if she'd ever made love to someone without there being some agenda.

For that matter, Michael wasn't sure he ever had that experience, either. Before the attack happened, sex was just sex. After the attack, sex was a game of skill and deception and illusion.

And lies.

"You want to kiss, then?" Michael asked. "Fine, then, let's suck face."

"Excuse me?"

"Make out. Swap spit."

Madeleine frowned. "Okay, that is not an appealing image and we can't. Not here."

"Why not?"

"We're in public."

Michael raised his arm around them. "We're in a dark movie theater with only two other people way over there. This is the perfect place to do it." He leaned over the armrest and he could see she wasn't backing away. For effect he wiggled his eyebrows. "You know you want to."

She must have, too, because when he dipped his head she didn't pull away. Their lips met and at first Michael kept it soft. A meeting of lips over and over again. A slow exploration of mouths. After a time she sighed and he pushed his tongue into her mouth, loving the feeling of penetrating her even if it was only this way. He thought about how nice this was. To kiss her and make love to her mouth and not worry about his moves for the coming steps ahead because there were no coming steps, and he didn't have to plan any other moves. He could sit here and neck all day with Madeleine Kane and be happy.

It was freeing. It was fun.

But then she reached her arm up and her fingers stroked along the edge of his chin and neck. He felt a ripple of sensation course through his body. Pulling away he could feel the puffs of air on his mouth. Although it was hard to see, he imagined her lips would be a little swollen and wet. Her eyes a little glassy.

He made her want him just by kissing her and he liked knowing that. This time she moved to him and started kissing him back. This time it was her tongue in his mouth and he had to hold back a groan of pleasure. Her mouth was wet and hot and so damn sexy. Need began to build and hunger tugged at his insides.

He was supposed to be enjoying this, simply taking in the feeling of two mouths meeting, but his body kicked in and told him it wanted more. It wanted everything. He wanted to consume Madeleine, become a part of her; let her become a part of him. He shifted a bit and deepened the angle of the kiss, letting his tongue clash with hers for supremacy. In his mind he saw her breasts naked in his palm; he saw her back arching as he thrust into her.

How could it be that he felt this good and was this turned on by a woman but not be hard?

As soon as the intrusive thought hit, any chance he had of letting his body relax ended. Because when he questioned his physical reaction he instantly went back to the reason behind it and in that dark place there was no pleasure. There was no peace.

He was about to end the kiss when a light flashed in his eyes.

"Hey, you two, break it up. This is a family theater."

Michael blinked and realized an old man wearing some sort of uniform was shining a flashlight down on them. Instinctively he held his hand up over Madeleine's face to protect her.

"Sorry," he mumbled.

"Geesh, and you two ain't even kids. Now what kind of example are you setting?"

Michael didn't bother to point out they weren't setting any example because there was no one behind them to see what they were doing.

"Sorry," he mumbled again.

"You two behave or I'm gonna...I'm gonna... I'm gonna get the manager!"

"Yes, sir."

With one last stern look, the usher eventually turned his flashlight back toward the floor as he moved down the aisle to secure the theater for all customers and prevent necking of any kind.

"I told you!" she whispered in his ear.

"Yeah, we got caught by the movie police. Oh, my!"

"This is not funny," she huffed.

On the contrary, he thought it was hysterically funny. Madeleine Kane got caught making out in a theater. He imagined that wasn't something that ever would have happened until she met him.

"Lighten up. We escaped with our lives."

This time she did chuckle and he enjoyed the sound so much he wrapped his arm around her shoulders, bringing the top half of her body closer to his so he could feel her humor.

"Michael?"

"Watch the movie before we really get in trouble."

"I want to say, the kissing… It was worth the risk."

He squeezed her arm and in response she rested her head against his shoulder.

Was it worth it? He didn't know. He wondered if every time he kissed her he was going to feel the stirrings of sexual arousal only to have some stray thought or memory plunge his body into a mental ice-cold bath.

This was definitely uncharted territory for him but he wasn't ready to give her up yet.

Not yet.

"ARE YOU ready to come home?"

Madeleine grasped her cell a little tighter. Michael had dropped her off back at her hotel and she'd been smiling like a goofy teenage girl who'd had the best date of her life. She wanted to take a hot shower and then crawl into bed, where hopefully she might dream about every delicious moment of the kiss they'd shared in the theater.

The question from Ben brought her spiraling back down to earth.

"Do you need me to come home? Did Anna leave you on your own?"

"Anna's still here. If not exactly happy about it," Ben added.

"Ben, tell me what happened. If it was a fight, you need to make up. Say you're sorry even if you don't mean it. You need her."

"I don't *need* anyone right now who isn't affiliated with the medical community, and I don't want to talk about Anna. I'm not calling you home to sit as a nurse on my sickbed.

You've been back in Detroit now for almost a week. I'm wondering if the assignment is over. I saw a Hollywood TV clip and they were actually extolling the charitable virtues of your boy without showing him plastered up against some starlet. I would say job well done."

"We've definitely made progress in a short amount of time. It's amazing how quickly a reputation can be made. Good or bad. In the twenty-four-hour cycle of news no one can remember what happened a month ago, so whatever the last impression is, that's the one that sticks."

"You were counting on that, no?"

She was. She realized she could safely say Michael Langdon was currently more thought of as a philanthropist than a playboy. Unfortunately, that didn't really give her any good reasons to stay in Detroit. At least none Ben would accept without questioning her.

"There is still the interview. I'll need to coach him through that, if it comes through."

"Isn't it likely to? That was Peg you dealt with at *Sunday Night Hour*. I know her. I can put in a call…"

"No—" Madeleine cut off her employer. For one, Ben didn't need to be doing anything extracurricular before his next round of treatment started. For another, Madeleine was no longer sure the interview was a good idea.

She knew Peg well enough to know she would do her research. She would spot the full three-year prison term as an anomaly. The attack would be on Michael's record. Maybe not the reason behind it, but she didn't want to put him in a situation where he would have to answer any questions regarding what had happened.

He could, of course, refuse to answer any questions regarding his time in prison. It wasn't unprecedented for an interviewee to dictate what the interviewer could and could not ask. But Madeleine knew too well how those interviews usually came off. Defensive. Guarded. As soon as people suspected you had something to hide they would press for more answers.

"You seem uncertain," Ben noted. "Do you have doubts about his ability to handle something like that?"

"No. And keep in mind we're not talking about a politician connecting with constituents. At the end of the day he's just a man looking to partner up with someone to make a really incredible car. I don't want you to worry about it, though. Peg will call in the next day or so to let me know."

"Wait. You said the car was really incredible. You've seen it?"

"I have." She smiled, knowing Ben's passion for all things automobile. "Basically, I can work it with my phone, drive it forever without impacting the environment and afford it on a couple of months of salary."

"Impressive. But does it fly?"

"He's still working on that."

Ben chuckled but Madeleine could sense his energy was fading. "You have to give me some sense of when you're coming back. I'm trying to get some…affairs in order. It would be easier if I knew your schedule and could have work lined up."

"Don't worry about my next assignment. Actually, I was thinking, maybe I might…take a couple of weeks…off."

She scrunched her face up, hoping she didn't sound so obvious. Thank goodness Ben avoided the FaceTime feature when he called her. She couldn't say why she was reluctant for him to know about her and Michael. Maybe in some ways she was afraid she would disappoint him by getting involved with yet another person she was working with.

When the silence lingered, she added, "It has been a while since I had a vacation."

"It's been five years by my count. The last time I brought it up you said, and I quote, 'vacation is for other people.' That's suddenly changed. Interesting. Also odd that you would choose Detroit as a vacation destination."

Really there was no point in the small deception. Trying to get something by Ben was like trying to sneak a big blow-up beach ball by an NHL hockey goalie. It wasn't going to happen. And deliberately not saying anything about it would make him think she felt guilty about the situation. Which she didn't. What was happening between her and Michael was like nothing that had happened between her and the president.

"What if I said Michael and I have become…friends? Very close friends."

There it was. On the table for her boss to deal with. His employee was forming a relationship with a person she was supposed to be working for. Technically, he could fire her. Worse, he could believe all those things that had once been said about her.

That she was power hungry. That she seduced men for the fun of it then spit them out. That she was someone who used sex for her own gain.

Please don't think any of those things. While it had been true…in that one awful moment…it wasn't who she was as a person.

But when he said nothing immediately she started on her defense. "Technically, our contract has ended. I'll only work with him again briefly if Peg does decide to do the interview. Otherwise our business relationship is over."

"And another relationship has taken its place."

"You disapprove," Madeleine said, trying to decipher if the low tone in his voice was disappointment or exhaustion.

"I'm not your father, Madeleine. And I'm not the public at large. You're one of the smartest women I know. As your employer, if you tell me your personal relationship has no impact on your professional one, then I don't give a shit what you and Michael Langdon do in private."

"Thank you."

"As your friend…I would remind you the man has a reputation you were paid to alter. I hope you don't confuse altering the impression with altering the man."

While Ben didn't understand the specifics, his words still struck home. She couldn't become invested with trying to change Michael. Or more accurately, fix Michael. If she was going to do this with him, she had to be willing to accept who he was in every way.

After all, he hadn't wanted to kiss her. She'd basically made him do that. What had he been thinking about before the usher arrived? That he was enjoying it or counting the minutes until it was over? No, he had to be enjoying it. She felt it. That kind of connection couldn't be faked.

How many times had he faked it with those other women?

Madeleine locked down the insidious thought and shook her head. "Trust me. I know what I'm doing." At least she hoped she did.

"Then I will. And if you need me, for anything, you know where to find me. It's not like I take a lot of detours between the house and the hospital."

"You promise me Anna is there with you."

"Anna…is here."

"Good luck," Madeleine offered, not sure what else to say. "Get better" seemed trite and overly optimistic.

"I'll need it."

She hung up the phone without saying goodbye. And without telling him how much he'd meant to her as a friend. If she started to speak those words she knew tears would follow and she didn't want to embarrass him. She knew Ben well enough to know that extreme emotion wasn't something he was comfortable with.

When her downfall occurred and she was being spun around in the aftermath of the scandal, like a small boat caught in a hurricane, there were days she wondered if she would ever be able to catch her breath again. Or if she would simply drown in humiliation.

She'd needed help back then. Her father would have nothing to do with her. Because his health was failing at the time, she understood why he couldn't be around her. Seeing her in his home only seemed to make him sicker, and the constant calls and press outside had only added to his strain.

And her brother was furious at her. For humiliating him, for putting their father through the stress and anguish of her debacle. But Madeleine always wondered if maybe deep down inside, Robert wasn't secretly thrilled to see the little sister who had surpassed him so fabulously come crashing back to earth.

Not the greatest sibling relationship.

No, it was only when Ben hired her and believed in her that the spinning had stopped.

He set her back on her feet and made her remember who she was. The person she'd been her whole life except for fifteen stupid minutes.

Not America's Jezebel. Not the Scandal of the Century. Not, as the First Lady once referred to her, the First Whore. Simply Madeleine Kane.

Madeleine thought about what Peg had said about losing Ben. It would be like losing God. If she did lose him, would it mean the spinning would start up again?

She hoped not. The waters were calmer now and after five years she liked to think she was stronger. More balanced.

Hadn't she kissed Michael in a public place?

That was daring for her. For others, that was the equivalent of walking down the middle of the street naked.

She still couldn't believe she'd agreed to it or that they were actually caught by an aging usher with a bright flashlight. Smiling to herself, she realized the whole adventure had been fun. And fun, much like vacation, was a concept she thought was more for others than for her. She liked it.

She liked it a lot.

CHAPTER TWELVE

"It's your turn."

"This is stupid." Michael looked at the cup filled with dice and wondered how it was a man could sink so low.

"It's Scrabble, it's not stupid."

They were sitting on the floor of her suite having finished their meal from room service. After a couple of days of dating Michael had quickly determined Madeleine's range of comfort and it didn't extend much further than her business range of comfort.

Dates could encompass movies; walks in the park, but only when Madeleine felt she was sufficiently camouflaged; lunch with Archie at Darnell's; and dinner at his house or room service in her suite. Anything else she deemed too "risky." And given that she thought walking through the park was putting things on the line, he knew any argument on the subject was pointless.

Not that he minded. Spending time with Madeleine any way he could was worth it. If he was a little disappointed that he couldn't impress her with fancy restaurants and trips on a private jet to New York, he'd dealt with it. Besides, he'd done those things with other women who had meant nothing to him and she might not like the idea of following in their footsteps. And it wasn't like Madeleine was the type to be impressed watching him spend his money, anyway.

But after they'd removed the remnants of their meal and the empty bottle of wine they'd shared out into the hall, she had suggested playing a game.

A board game. It was emasculating—or it would have been if he hadn't already been emasculated. Because one of the problems with not being able to take her to a show or a restaurant or a sporting event meant much of the time they spent together was alone and in private.

When a man was alone with a woman he wanted… in private…certain thoughts came to mind. Maybe she thought she was helping sidestep the issue of sex in their relationship, but in his mind all she was doing was calling it into sharp focus.

Things were becoming increasingly difficult in that area. Each time they said hello or good-night, they started kissing and it was like setting sparks on dry kindle. He felt his body react in ways he didn't think he would ever feel again. Always to be followed by the plummeting realization he couldn't take what he wanted because his body would ultimately betray him. Their passion could only go so far before it would stop. He left her wanting and unsatisfied and even though she denied it, he knew it had to be frustrating.

Hell, he was frustrated.

Michael was beginning to think it was time to change that. After all, there were many other ways for her to achieve sexual release. At least one of them should be able to get off. He was about to say something when her cell chirped from her desk.

"Leave it," he urged her.

"Can't. Could be Ben." Unraveling her legs from the twist she'd arranged them in, Michael watched as she gracefully transitioned from sitting to standing in a way a man never could.

Knowing they were staying in, she'd worn stretchy yoga pants and a soft, well-worn sweatshirt. Her hair was pulled into a careless ponytail and her face was clean of any makeup he could see.

He thought her more stunning than any of the models or starlets he'd ever dated. The fact that her feet were bare and he could see her toes were painted ridiculously pink made him feel like a king for being allowed into her inner sanctum.

She was maddening to him. Seemingly within his grasp, but still out of reach.

"Hey, Peg. Okay, great. I'll run it by him and then we'll talk about scheduling. Thanks."

She turned back to him with her bottom lip between her teeth and he instantly had ideas about replacing her teeth with his. He could, he had, nibbled on that mouth for hours.

"What?"

"Peg wants to do the interview. Her boss is excited about the idea."

Michael leaned back on the couch behind him. "You don't look excited by the idea. I thought this was what you wanted."

"It was. I think it's a great opportunity to show not only who you are but what the car is about. People are going to be interested. Not just people in the automotive industry, but I bet the government, as well. They've been trying to push electric cars for years, but the demand isn't there. You can change all that and create a new demand."

"So what's the problem?"

"No problem," she said slowly. "Maybe a concern. Peg is one of the best at what she does. She'll dig. She'll dig real deep. So will whoever is actually going to do the interview."

Immediately Michael understood. "You're worried she'll find out the truth."

"She'll find out about the attack and why you served the full three years. There is no doubt about that."

"I've covered my tracks, Madeleine. Very well. She'll find out about the assault but not why I initiated it. Prisoners get into fights all the time. It happens."

"And you're going to be okay talking about it?"

"Sure," he joked. "I love to talk about it. It's my favorite thing in the world. Ask me anything about my time in jail. I'll tell you about the food and the chores and what it's like to sleep on a cot you're too big for."

She walked over to him and knelt next to him. "I'm serious. This isn't something you have to do if you don't want to."

"You said it's the best way to attract attention. That's what this whole shindig was about, remember?"

"I remember." She sighed.

"It's going to be okay," he promised her. At least he hoped it was going to be okay. Thoughts of Nooky emerged, but Michael believed he'd scared the guy off for good. He hadn't seen or heard a word from him since that day at the park nearly a week ago. Although he probably should check in with Archie to see if the rat had quit his job. He made a mental note to follow up.

No, he didn't think Nooky was the issue. The question was, how many more like him were out there? How many more times would some rat come find him and threaten to tell everyone all his secrets?

Inwardly Michael shrugged. He didn't know, but it was his cross to bear. It was the one thing he kept going back to anytime he took a moment to feel sorry for himself. Everything that happened, the attack, his sexual issues as a result of it, the people like Nooky who would forever stink up his life, all of it was because of what he'd done.

He'd made the choice to steal the car. He'd done that and no one else.

"Do you want to keep playing?"

Michael looked at the abandoned game pieces and rubbed his hand over his face. "No, I don't want to play a game anymore."

"Can I ask a question instead?"

Inwardly he tensed. Somehow he knew this wasn't going to be good. "Okay."

She settled against him on the floor and

being comfortable enough there he didn't think to move.

"How did you do it? How did you change?"

"You mean, how did I escape becoming a career criminal? That's easy. After I beat the crap out of Ricca…"

It was funny to him. It was a name he hadn't allowed himself to think of in years. Hadn't even thought of it until Nooky wrote it in a note and now he'd said it. Out loud. He waited for the memories first, then the crippling sense of shame, but there was nothing. Only Madeleine pressed against his side waiting for some magic answer as to how he turned his life around.

He didn't know how magic it was, but it was the truth.

"After the fight, I spent the next two weeks in solitary. I thought about what would happen if he died. I mean, it would be murder, right? Maybe manslaughter, whatever, but I knew if he died it meant I was going to have to spend the rest of my life in prison. I couldn't do that, so I was going to kill myself."

She made a small sound, not quite a gasp, more like a hiss.

"And it wasn't the teenage melodramatic kind of thought. I mean, I knew deep down that this was it. I couldn't do it for life. Which meant I wouldn't live if he didn't live. When I got out of solitary they told me he woke up from the coma. He didn't appear to have any lasting brain damage and in a few weeks would probably be fine. So now I was going to live. Not die, but live. I thought to myself… you got your life back, asshole. Now what are you going to do with it?"

She bumped his shoulder with her own. "You shouldn't use that kind of language."

He laughed at that. "Sorry. I forget I'm dealing with Miss Ivy League over here."

"So you had a rebirth and decided you were going to change everything."

He looked at her then. "Not at first. Had you asked me then I probably would have told you my plan was to be a better car thief and not get caught. Over the years that changed. I kept to myself pretty much but I would hear guys talk in the yard and whatever work assignment I was on. Everyone I knew or heard about was a do-over."

"Do over?"

"Do-over," he explained, "is when you commit the crime, do the time, then do it over again."

"Career criminals," she surmised.

"They couldn't learn. I used to get so frustrated. Why didn't they learn? If you were a house robber and you got caught and you were back in jail for robbing a house then you obviously didn't figure out how not to get caught. Idiots. Then it hit me, the only way not to get caught was to not do it in the first place. That's when I knew if I was going to really make it out of that place and never go back, I was going to have to figure out another way to earn a living."

"That's a good story," she said. "You tell whoever is interviewing you that story and you might change some lives."

"It's a crap story, Madeleine." He didn't want to paint a pretty picture, at least not with her, that he was the bad boy who had turned everything around. A feel-good ending to a hard-luck case, which is what all the stories about him portrayed. With her he had always been honest and he didn't want to back away from that.

"That experience ruined me."

She nodded and rested her chin on his shoulder in support. "Yep, in one way. But it also made you, in another way. How's that for irony?"

Eff irony, he thought. But he didn't say the word out loud because Madeleine didn't like bad language.

For a time they sat there together, until the restlessness inside him kicked in. He stood. "I'm going to head out."

"Don't," she said. "Stay and have another drink. We'll be bad and order up another bottle of wine."

He smiled at her version of bad. "I can't do that. I have to drive home."

"Then stay…the night." Immediately she rose onto her knees and shuffled around until she was in front of him. It was erotic since she looked so earnest.

"Madeleine…"

"Is it wrong for me to ask? I mean, I thought we could sleep together. Just sleep. I haven't done that in a very long time."

He hadn't done it ever. He'd never been much of a cuddler, anyway, and the lingering fear of having his partner turn to him the next morning expecting him to have an early morning boner was enough to make sure he left before any sleeping happened.

But this was Madeleine and she was sort of begging on her knees.

Every instinct he had told him this was a bad idea.

"Okay."

CHAPTER THIRTEEN

"ARE YOU READY?" she called from the bathroom adjacent to the bedroom.

Michael looked around the empty hotel room not sure what to expect. He certainly hoped she wasn't about to put on some sexy show. That would only be embarrassing for both of them.

They had decided on the second bottle of wine. It was the only way he was going to make it through another round of Scrabble. The result was Madeleine knew a lot of crazy words and they were both slightly tipsy.

She more so, which made him wonder about what she was about to come out of that bathroom wearing. Maybe something see-through would be fun, after all.

He'd undressed down to his boxer briefs and was now taking off his watch to leave on the bed stand. It seemed such a natural thing for a man to do but inside he was nervous as hell.

"Michael?"

He'd forgotten he was supposed to answer. "Yeah, yeah," he said and sat on the edge of the bed.

The door to the bathroom opened and the bathroom light filtered around her. She'd gone with an oversize T-shirt and a pair of cotton shorts. No peekaboo nightie, but he thought this outfit was just as sexy. Her hair was still tied back in a loose ponytail and he could smell the faint hint of mint from the toothpaste she'd used.

If he'd been asked when he first met her what kind of pajamas did he imagine Madeleine Kane would wear, he would have said something sleek, cool and sexy. Elegant silk in deep rich colors.

The more he was coming to know her, the more he realized how far away she was from that cool facade he'd first met. He smiled thinking about the way she'd sat across from him on that first meeting so prim and professional. The way she could show cool disdain with simply the lift of an eyebrow.

He'd wanted her then. Wanted to put her on a pedestal and worship her forever.

But he wanted this version more, this flawed and contradictory woman. This was the woman only he got to see. He sensed he was among very few people in her life who had the privilege.

"No shirt?" Her voiced faltered a bit and he wondered if she was as nervous as he was.

"I didn't think to pack pajamas and I sure as hell am not wearing yours."

She smiled. "I guess that doesn't work in reverse, does it?"

"No. Come here."

She walked over to him and he opened his legs to allow her closer. He ran his hands over her bottom and rested his head against her chest, finding a home there he hadn't known he'd been looking for. Her fingers ran through his hair and then rested on his shoulders. The nerves faded a bit.

"Can I kiss you?" she wanted to know.

He lifted his head. "You can always kiss me."

Moving out from between his legs, she crawled onto the bed and lay down on her side facing him. "Then come kiss me."

Michael lay down. "I thought you said you wanted to kiss me."

"I guess I did." She undulated toward him, moving her body as close as she could. Her leg slipped between his and she cupped his cheek with her hand.

He was in a pool of Madeleine and he didn't want to get out.

"Thank you for staying with me," she whispered before pressing her lips against his.

The trick, Michael learned, was to stay in his head. As long as he could remain there it stopped him from feeling the rush of pleasure, which came every time they touched. He didn't want the pleasure anymore. At first it had been alluring, even tempting, to think that it might change something or lead to something more. But the crash and fall were always too disappointing.

So he kissed her and he used his lips and his tongue but inside, mentally, he was putting letters together to form unappealing words.

Burp. Dirt. Jail.

But then she sighed into his mouth and her leg shifted up over his thigh. Instinctively he pulled her closer, his hand reaching for her bottom to bring her into full contact with his body. He felt her breasts against his chest. Soft mounds of flesh highlighted with hard tips poking through the cotton of her shirt and marking his chest.

Her hands were on his back and he realized this was the first time she'd touched him, skin on skin. It was electric. Like he was truly being touched for the first time in years. As if he'd been nothing more than a ghost walking among substantial people. Through her touch he felt himself coming back to life. He could feel her fingers, her palm...the tip of a nail gently tracing a path down his spine.

Don't think about how good she feels in your arms. Don't think about her tongue teasing your ear or her lips pressed against your neck.

Don't think.

It was all feeling too good. Suddenly he was a man in bed with his woman after a nice night and they were going to make love. He was going to sit her up and pull her T-shirt over her head.

He tossed the shirt to the floor.

He was going to cup her breasts and lower his head to suck on a hard nipple.

Her moans echoed in the hotel room, growing louder as his mouth grew bolder.

He was going to tug her cotton shorts down her long legs, letting his fingers graze the underside of her knees.

She bent her legs when he touched the sensitive skin there and then he flipped the shorts over his shoulder and they, too, landed on the floor.

She was naked. She was underneath him. He had everything in the world he wanted.

Except an erection.

On his knees, his weight braced on his hands while he held himself above her, he looked down at his body. There was a change. He could feel the rush of blood to his groin and if he was being generous with himself, he might have said he was semihard. But it wasn't enough to get him where he wanted.

Deep inside her. He needed that now. Not for the sake of the sexual release, but for the connection to her. He wanted them locked together. Her fingers reached up and caught in the waistband of his briefs. Immediately he pulled her hands away and pinned them against his abs.

"No," he said. He didn't want her to see him in this state. His body in a death match with his memories. "Madeleine, I brought a pill with me."

"What?"

She was still in the middle of a sexual haze, twisting her body on the sheets in an instinctive gesture to her lover that she was ready to be filled by him.

So beautiful.

"A pill. In my wallet. Let me get it. I want to be inside you. I want to take you...hard. I can do that with the pill. I can satisfy you that way."

The haze seemed to clear from her eyes and she stilled on the bed. Blinking, she pulled her hands out of his grasp and focused on him still kneeling above her. "No. I don't want that."

"Why not?" he snapped. "What difference does it make? We can make love. I can make you come so many times..."

"But you can't. So it's not real. I don't want that."

He gritted his teeth in frustration. "Fine. If you won't let me come inside you that way, we'll do it another way."

Moving down her body, he put his mouth on her bare stomach. Her skin was so soft, so incredibly luscious. What would she be like between her slick folds? It would blow his mind and he would get his tongue and his fingers so deep inside her that when she came he would feel it throughout his body, as well.

His tongue slipped into her belly button, then he dipped his head farther. In the dim moonlight shining in between the hotel-room curtains, he could see the glistening slickness of her arousal on the soft dark curls between her thighs.

"No."

She wiggled and the motion made him crazy because it put her sex farther away from his mouth. She was going to make him work for it.

He dipped his head again.

"No. I said no." She pushed against his shoulder.

Lifting his head, Michael saw her expression and knew suddenly she wasn't feeling it anymore. "I want to go down on you."

"I know what you're doing," she said, clearly annoyed with him for thinking her that naive.

"Don't you...like it?" He didn't think it was possible for a woman not to like it. Like it wasn't possible for a man to not like getting his dick sucked. Some things were a given.

"It's not that. I don't feel comfortable with this being so one-sided. I mean, I'll be...I'll be into it...but you'll just be watching."

Michael rose up to face her. "I'll be doing a hell of a lot more than just watching. I'm okay with this, Madeleine. I want to make you come. Giving you pleasure pleasures me. And as a man I can't believe I actually said those words, but in this case, in your case, it's the truth."

She scooted back on the bed, leaning on the headboard as she curled her knees into her chest.

"I'm sorry," she said stiffly. "I'm not okay with it."

He stared at her a minute, dumbfounded, until a wave of sharp and nasty anger rose up inside him. "What the...?"

She flinched, sensing he was about to swear, and so he said the word he wanted even louder. Glad to make her flinch. He was that kind of angry.

"You won't let me use a pill. Which would work perfectly fine. And you won't let me go down on you. Why? You have a thing against orgasms."

"I don't have a *thing* against orgasms. I thought we were going to..."

"What? What did you think we were going to do? We start kissing and things get hot between us. Inferno hot. I can't follow through, I get that, but it doesn't mean we can't do other things or use the freakin' pill and—"

"And pretend! That's what you were going to say and I don't want to pretend anything with you. It would be dishonest and it's not what we have together."

He could practically see her mind spinning as she worked to find words that would explain what had no explanation. She thought she could talk her way out of this. She probably thought she could talk her way out of anything. Only she must not have been able to think of something remotely reasonable because all she did was squeeze her knees tighter to her chest.

"You know what I think? I think you are more messed up about intimacy than either of us realized. You don't like sex."

"That's not true! You know how untrue it is. You felt how…that I was…excited."

"Yeah, because your body can't help the physical reaction. But in that little head of yours you're thinking all the time and I think you don't want this because you don't like being the one out of control."

That had her head snapping toward him. He'd struck a nerve, and instead of backing off he did what any good fighter from the other side of the tracks did, he pressed his advantage and fought even dirtier.

"You don't know what sex is when it's not a commodity, do you? People used you, you used people. Was it ever fun for you? Did you ever want to screw for the sake of it?"

"Stop it."

She was shaking now. He could see her body practically trembling and it didn't make him feel good to know he'd done that to her. Fighting dirty was great, but not when it meant hurting someone he...

He what?

Don't think. Don't even let the word form in your head. At the end of the day this can go nowhere. Tonight proved that, if nothing else.

"I'm sorry," he mumbled as he searched the floor for her clothes. He tossed her the shirt and shorts and felt another little jab when she quickly wiggled back into them.

"I'm leaving." He walked over to the chair where he'd draped his slacks and the cashmere sweater he'd worn.

"So that's it. I won't put out and you're leaving. Real mature."

Stepping into his pants, he fastened them and set his buckle in place. "That's not what this is about and you know it."

"No, tell me." Dressed now, she was more confident. She slid off the bed and stood in front of him. "I didn't feel comfortable with what you wanted to do. That's all it was."

No, it was more than that. She didn't want to be vulnerable in front of him. Didn't want to be exposed in a way he wouldn't be. Because deep down, they wouldn't be feeling the same things. He should have been more understanding, maybe. This couldn't be any easier for her than it was for him.

Yet, she had to acknowledge, he'd been exposed and vulnerable in front of her every time he'd been with her since she'd learned the truth about his past.

He was giving her everything. She wasn't giving it back in return.

"Madeleine." He reached up and cupped her face. Her pretty eyes were brimming with so much fear. "I don't know who you are trying to kid, me or yourself. You need to think about this. Is it me you really want to be with? Or is it a hell of a lot easier having a relationship with a guy who can't get it up? No way to be out of control in that scenario, now is there?"

His hand dropped and he turned away from her to put on his sweater. Finding his shoes, he stepped into them.

"You shouldn't drive."

"I won't. I'll grab a cab."

Nodding, she wrapped her arms around her middle, protecting herself as much as she could. He wanted to tell her that she didn't have to protect herself from him. That with him she was safe. But he was coming to learn that Madeleine had never trusted anyone. Not really. It made him inexplicably sad.

Her bottom lip trembled a bit before she lifted her chin. "So is this it?"

It. The end.

It probably should be. Michael couldn't see how this was ever going to get any better between them. Not when she was in this much denial and he was…still broken. But he couldn't make himself say the words. The idea of never seeing her again simply wasn't an option.

Still, she had a choice in this, too. "Do you want it to be?"

"No," she answered instantly.

Despite everything that had happened, her quick response made him feel good. "Then no, this isn't it. But you're going to have to think about why you won't let yourself be naked with me."

"I was naked!" she answered shrilly.

"That wasn't naked. You forgot to take your armor off."

With that he snatched up his watch and left the room trying real hard to forget the look of horror he saw on her face.

Yeah…he was a dirty fighter.

MADELEINE WANTED TO hurl something at his back. A lamp or a vase or something that would make him hurt the way he'd hurt her.

Armor? How dare he? How could he? She'd never been so vulnerable before.

Hell, she'd never been completely naked with any man ever before.

Falling back on the bed, she groaned as the deep insidious voice inside her head worked its way up and out of her mouth. Never having let herself be fully naked with a man probably wasn't a good defense against his argument.

"He's right. Oh, God." Covering her face with her hands, this time she wanted to hurl something at herself.

Idiot! Fool! Stupid!

He was completely right. She was so messed up in the head about sex and she was sick of it. How many years had she been blaming the *scandal?* Not that it could be trivialized. What woman wouldn't be traumatized by being caught in the act by a scorned wife who'd labeled her the country's First Whore?

But she knew it went deeper than that. A memory she'd long suppressed came crashing down on her. She could practically hear his snide voice in her head even after all these years.

That's right. I got into Madeleine Kane's pants. Not so high and mighty now, is she? I've checked her off the list. Now, who's next?

He'd been a boy. Kevin. Her first boy. She'd met him in debate class at Yale and fallen so hard and fast she didn't think she would ever recover. She'd laughed with him, been enthralled by him, and despite how humiliating it was to admit now, she'd even pretended he was smarter than her.

Of course she'd given him her virginity. Lights out, bra still on, with as much courage as she could summon. It hadn't been easy. She'd been raised to be a good girl.

To her very proper, very traditional family, sex outside of marriage was not only a sin, but it was also a distraction. Boys and parties and fun were the enemies of discipline.

Madeleine supposed that had to do with living with two men. Her father certainly had drilled into her nothing more than a steady regimen of study and an unwavering focus on preparing for her future. Anything else was superfluous. Her brother, Robert, was no better in that regard, either. But with him it was always a competition. Who had the higher GPA? Who was winning more awards? Certainly, Robert never veered from the course and still, even he spent his Saturday nights out with friends or girls.

The very thought of her bringing a boy home to meet either of them had been ludicrous to her in high school.

Maybe it would have been different if her mother had lived; maybe there could have been room for some balance in her life. Boys and clothes and dances. But there was no changing her past.

It was her naïveté that made her such an easy target for Kevin.

She'd been willing to do anything to keep him. So she'd fought with her modesty and her guilt over doing something she felt was innately wicked, and she'd had sex with him. She made him actually show her the condom he was going to use to ensure she wouldn't get pregnant, never once telling him she was already on the pill, as she'd felt two precautions would be more effective than one. Eventually he'd become impatient with her, then finally frustrated with her lack of enthusiasm when she didn't seem to be able to relax and enjoy it.

It was only her unwillingness to fail at anything that finally saw the deed done.

The next day, she'd overheard him in the hallway before debate class telling his friend what he'd accomplished. The conversation they had was very detailed as he revealed deep and personal information about her. By the end of it she'd been cured of any feelings she'd had for him.

She'd been played. She certainly wasn't the first woman. Hell, she doubted she was his first woman. What drove her mad was how stupid she'd been. How oblivious she was to every sign. Why had he pursued her so doggedly? Why was it that he loved absolutely everything she loved? Every movie, every restaurant. He had even loved sneaking into extra lectures that weren't on their class list, which was her way of being bad. All of it had been a coordinated effort by him to check her off his list.

The sex had brought her down a peg, she knew. The only thing that gave her any peace about the whole ordeal was that while she'd been pretending to be his intellectual inferior, he'd known the truth. He'd known she was smarter and that's why he had targeted her.

Madeleine figured most girls were able to shrug it off. Chalk it up to the guy being an asshole and move on to the next boy. But beyond his strict teachings, her father had also drilled in her a demand for excellence. It didn't matter that she'd had no real chance to flirt or date in high school. It should have come naturally, like some built-in gift.

She should have been better with boys. More secure, more confident, more...aware of what their actions meant. She shouldn't have ever been targeted as a candidate for humiliation.

To do anything that could be held to ridicule was unthinkable.

The humiliation that was so much a part of her first sexual experience dogged her throughout college. She'd grown harder, colder, more closed off. Not exactly a man magnet when there were so many other willing coeds to choose from.

When she'd started working, she was the new kid on the political circuit. Older, more mature men had seen all that aloofness she wrapped herself in and taken it as a challenge. And because she wanted to be free from her sexual prison, she let a few persuade her back into the bedroom. But the trust was never there and the people she'd been with seemed to know it.

All of those experiences culminated in that last awful one. The one where she'd decided maybe she could be the user instead of the used. Maybe she could finally get what she wanted out of sex.

Michael had been so right. About all of it.

Stripping away all the denials and lies, she had to ask herself if what made him so compelling to her was the fact that he was impotent. Maybe she thought the two of them could drift along in platonic complacency forever.

But no, that first night before she had known his secrets she had wanted him and had been willing to take the risk of going to bed with him. It had been like stepping off a high cliff. Part of her knew hitting bottom might be crushing, but she also knew the ride down could be worth it. With him.

Then he'd confessed.

Initially, it had seemed like such a perfect match on paper. He would be content with whatever she had to give because of what he couldn't physically give her. And she could accept everything that he was giving her without worrying if he was ever going to want too much.

Only he wasn't happy. He wanted to be with her. He wanted to pleasure her. He wanted her to lay herself completely bare before him.

A low groan emanated from her throat. It sounded a lot like self-disgust.

Her ringing cell phone broke through her

self-disdain. She wanted to ignore it, but knew she couldn't. It could be Ben.

Or it could be Michael.

Calling her to tell her…what? That he was sorry? Hardly a reason to do that when she was in the wrong.

Walking out into the suite, she picked up the phone she'd left on her desk.

Anna's name blinked up at her. Instantly she answered. "Anna. What is it?"

"It's Ben," Anna said, her voice cracking as she spoke. "He's going to try to kill himself."

CHAPTER FOURTEEN

MADELEINE STRODE DOWN the hospital hallway with purpose toward the visitors' waiting room. She stopped when she saw Anna
sitting there, alone in the room except for another woman who sat quietly in the corner
with her knitting. To say Anna looked dev-
astated was an understatement.

Anna stood and walked toward her with
less-than-steady steps. Madeleine met her
halfway with her arms open. She embraced
the younger woman and held her while she
cried.

"What happened?"

"He's a stubborn jackass. That's what happened."

"Anna, talk to me. You scared the hell out
of me last night when you told me. I've been
scrambling ever since to get back here as
soon as possible."

Madeleine guided Anna into two seats.

"He wasn't happy with how the treatment

was going," Anna said dully. "And you know Ben—all or nothing."

Madeleine could feel the hair on her arms stand up. She did know Ben and she didn't like the sound of Anna's voice. "What's he doing?"

"A radical chemo treatment followed by radiation to kill off the cancer followed by a bone-marrow transplant."

Madeleine gasped. She didn't have to ask Anna why she was so scared. They had all done the research on his condition. A bone-marrow transplant was incredibly risky if Ben's body rejected it. Graft-versus-host disease was deadly. And the chance of contracting GVHD without having a close genetic match was that much higher.

"Whose marrow? Ben has no family that I know of."

"Exactly. His parents are dead. I found a second cousin in Boston, but he isn't nearly close enough for a genetic match. And the odds of finding a match through the donor program are like hitting the lottery."

"Which leaves him only one option," Madeleine said, thinking back to the articles she had read.

"Yep. He's going to use cells from an umbilical cord. The idea is the cells are so new the body might accept them better."

"I take it you're not happy with his choice."

Anna's head dropped into her hands. "He could have done another round of chemo, something stronger. He could have waited until the results of that came through before even considering doing this. The doctors talked about four levels of treatment, this being the most extreme. Ben was only through round one. He didn't have to do this."

"Why is he?"

Anna laughed without any humor. Leaning back against the hard chair, she closed her eyes and breathed deeply. Madeleine patiently waited for her to gather herself. That something had happened between these two was evident. What she was witnessing wasn't distress or even sorrow. Anna was on full-blown meltdown.

"He said he was done with being sick. He was either going to be cured or he was going to die, but he was done *playing.* Playing."

"I'm sorry, Anna. It sounds like Ben."

"It does. I wouldn't even have known what he'd decided if I hadn't checked with his doctor about the week's schedule. I was bringing him in so early on Friday it didn't smell right. That's when the doctor said they were checking him in indefinitely. He's going through the chemo now. Then they'll do the radiation treatment. After that, in a couple of days, they'll do the transplant. Then he has to remain in a solitary ICU for at least forty-five days to prevent infection."

"Can we visit him during that time?"

She shook her head. "No. They won't let us in the room. We can see him distantly through the glass walls, but we can't get close enough to actually speak to him."

"We'll send messages with the nurses," Madeleine said, trying to comfort her. "We'll let him know we're here. That he has our support."

"No, *we* won't." Anna shook her head. "I called you because I can't leave him alone. Of all the people on his team, you seem to be the closest. I know you consider him a friend."

"He is my friend. He's your friend, too."

"No. He's not my friend."

"Anna..."

"We made love," she blurted. "No, sorry. I made love. He had sex."

Madeleine said nothing. Anna swallowed, then met her gaze directly. "Did you know how I felt about him?"

"I guessed." Madeleine sighed. "I think it was one of those things I knew but didn't want to go there. You work so closely together, and I didn't know how it would work out for you two. But I will say, I've never seen him let anyone get that close. I thought maybe...he felt the same way about you."

"He doesn't."

"How do you know? You said you two made love. That means he was attracted to you. He wanted you."

"Nope," she said abruptly. "He realized that what he was about to do might kill him. I think he wanted one last roll in the hay while he could still get it up. It's not like he could go trolling the bars looking for an easy pickup. And of course, hookers and their possible contaminants were out of the question. I was nothing more than convenient."

Madeleine closed her eyes against the bitterness in Anna's voice, knowing it wasn't borne out of truth, but instead out of Anna's pain. "You can't say that. Is that what you were fighting about? When I walked in on you two?"

"I wanted to go with him to the doctor's. I wanted to be there to discuss his next course of treatment. He wouldn't let me. Said it was none of my business. When I politely brought up the fact that we were sort of lovers now, and that made a difference, he made his feelings completely clear. 'It just happened…' That's what he said. 'It doesn't change anything.'"

Madeleine didn't believe it, but she didn't think Anna was in any state to hear that. Sex changed everything. Especially between two people as close as Anna and Ben.

"Anyway, I can't stay. The doctors said they should know in a month if his body will accept the bone marrow or not. I can't wait around and see if he's going to live. I can't do it. I can't stand here day in and day out looking through some glass at a man lying in a hospital bed, maybe dying, who made this choice without me. I love him, but he doesn't love me back. So I can't stay."

"Anna, you don't want to do something you might regret."

"You don't know me. I've lost too many people in my life to go through this again. He knew it, too. So I'm done with *playing,* too, and I won't regret anything."

Sensing she needed to tread very softly, Madeleine nodded. She didn't want to alienate Anna, because she knew if Anna left right now she would need a path back someday. The least Madeleine could do was be that path for her.

"Okay. Is there anything you want me to tell him?"

Anna stood and waited a moment as if testing to see if her legs would hold her. "Yes, please. Tell him I quit."

With that she left the waiting area and didn't once look back.

OVER THE NEXT few days Madeleine spent most of her time going between Ben's home and the hospital, only stopping at her place to shower and change clothes.

Being Anna, she had found a temporary replacement to handle Ben's business correspondence and had already hired a nurse to help him through his recovery once he returned home. His house had been cleaned and sanitized and was ready for him. Madeleine had inspected all the work and was satisfied with it.

She spent part of her days touching base with each of her coworkers to give them an update on Ben's condition. The rest of her days were spent doing as Anna had asked of her—being there for Ben. Although she couldn't say how much he registered her presence. The chemo had left him weak and nauseous and, according to the nurses, as irritable as a bear with a thorn in his paw.

Standing outside the ICU unit, Madeleine could finally see Ben through a glass partition as they settled him into his bed. Ben had undergone the marrow transplant and was recovering. He looked whiter than the sheets he was lying on, but he was alert and speaking with the doctor. He'd looked over once and saw her standing there. She'd smiled and waved, and when he'd turned his head away she could almost feel his disappointment. It had been several days and Anna hadn't shown herself once. Ben had to realize what that meant.

When the nurse came out, Madeleine waited for any kind of update.

"He feels pretty lousy," she said. "Not really much to be done about that but to keep him as comfortable as possible. Now we wait and see if the bone marrow will take."

"I understand. Can he have his tablet in the room with him or his phone so I can talk with him?"

"Maybe tomorrow when he's a little stronger. Right now he needs rest more than anything. Are you Anna?"

"No."

The nurse clearly looked uncomfortable.

"It's okay," Madeleine assured her, sensing

the woman feared she had ratted out her patient. "I'm a friend. Anna is another friend."

Relieved, the nurse nodded. "He was asking for her, is all."

Madeleine nodded. She had no intention of letting him know she had quit. Although, given her absence, he had to suspect it. The reality could wait until he felt better. For now, let him think that she was only upset with him and that was why she wasn't visiting.

Not knowing what else to do, Madeleine made her way back to the waiting area.

She thought of Anna who had done this for days on end alone while he'd been undergoing his first round of chemo treatment. Of course she must have loved him. The question was, did Ben know? For a very smart businessman, it wouldn't surprise her if he was obtuse in other areas of his life.

In that way they were similar.

Of course Madeleine had called Michael to let him know where she was going and that she would be needed in Philadelphia for several weeks. He'd offered to come with her but she had refused. Things were still too uncertain between them. Asking him to do nothing but be support for her seemed selfish.

And the separation would be a good thing, she told herself. She could spend the time waiting around in the hospital thinking about him, about their relationship and about her obvious trust issues. When she was around him, all rational thought seemed to fly out the door. Without him here, she could really focus. This would be good for them. This would help put their feelings in perspective. This would allow them to objectively evaluate if they were simply two people who had become friends or if they were something more and what that would mean between them sexually.

Yes, being without him seemed like a very practical idea.

When she got back to the waiting area, the woman who sat quietly knitting wasn't alone. At the other end of the room sat Michael. In a pair of jeans and a comfortable sweater, he looked as good as anything she had ever seen in her life.

All her grand ideas about wanting separation from him evaporated like water in a steam room. The way they had left each other, even the awkwardness during their phone call when she'd told him not to come, all of it meant nothing.

He was here.

He stood and opened his arms and like she'd never before done in her life, she ran to him and threw herself into him. She held him as if she would never let go.

"You came," she whispered on his neck.

"Yep."

"I told you that you didn't have to."

"You told me not to," he corrected her. Then he pulled back and looked into her face. "I don't like being told what to do. Besides, I missed you."

And she'd missed him. They had been apart for a couple of days, and she hadn't realized that she'd felt like a piece of her was missing until she'd seen him again and knew what that piece was.

She was in trouble. Big-time, deep-down trouble. Because she was starting to suspect she was in love with him and it scared the crap out of her.

"Have you seen him?"

"Yes, through glass. He's not allowed any visitors. He looks…well, not great. But he's awake and alert. The nurse said all we can do now is wait and see how his body responds to the bone marrow."

"If I know Ben, he's probably willing his body into submission right now. He'll intimidate it into doing whatever he commands."

Madeleine smiled.

"Do you want to stay here for a while?"

She shook her head. "I wanted to see him after the treatment. But now he'll sleep for the rest of the day. We can leave."

Since Michael had taken a cab from the airport to the hospital, Madeleine drove. She looked for signs that he was uneasy being a passenger instead of a driver, but he didn't seem to mind. In fact, he rested his head back against the seat, and for a moment, Madeleine thought he might have dozed off.

"How far to your place?" he asked out of nowhere.

"Uh, not far. I'm only about fifteen minutes outside the city."

Of course she was taking him back to her home. It only made sense he would stay with her. They were two people in a relationship. She had plenty of room. Yes, absolutely, it was the only choice. So why did she feel so afraid?

When she glanced over to see if this time he was actually sleeping, she could see that instead he was staring back at her. Assessing her.

"If you don't want me to stay with you, just drop me off at a hotel."

"Don't be ridiculous. Of course I want you to stay with me. Why would you suggest I don't?"

"Because when I asked about your place you got as stiff as a board."

Madeleine forced herself to relax but it was too late. She shook her head and laughed.

"What's so funny?"

"Me. And me with you. I remember being on the phone with you once and I freaked out because I wasn't wearing shoes."

"Shoes?"

"We were talking about work. It was a professional call and when I work or interact with anyone I'm always properly dressed. Armor in place and all that, but I was being slightly rebellious and had removed my shoes. Then you wanted to do FaceTime and I panicked."

Michael sighed. "I'm sorry about the armor comment. You know where I come from. Sometimes I fight dirty."

"You were right, though. I have...issues."

This time Michael chuckled.

"Don't laugh at me, I'm coming clean here."

"Lady, you didn't want me to go down on you and give you an orgasm. It doesn't take a rocket scientist to figure out you have issues. But I get the sense you admitting them out loud is a big deal. Hell, I know how big a deal admitting my issues was. We're even in that regard."

Madeleine squirmed a bit, but he was right. If she was going to come clean about everything, she figured she owed him the truth about why she was shaking in her boots over the idea of him staying in her house with her.

She took the exit off the Schuylkill Expressway for City Line Avenue. A few more turns and she was driving up a small incline of a road and then onto her driveway. She lifted her hand to the sun visor and hit the button on the small remote. The gate to her driveway slid back, allowing the car to enter.

With the fence, the house was completely obscured from the road. On two carefully landscaped acres of land, it was also invisible to any of her neighbors. Only someone who had gotten past the gate and reached the top of the driveway would know a house was there.

She drove up to the house, turned off the engine and sat for a moment. Michael didn't ask her why she wasn't moving and he didn't make any moves to get out, either. Instead he reached over and grabbed her hand. The contact was warm and comforting and reminded her why she'd gone from leaving off her shoes while talking to him to this moment of intimacy.

"I mean it. If you're uncomfortable with this I can go to a hotel."

"No. I am not going to lie. I am uncomfortable with this, but I want you here. I'm afraid you'll think I'm insane. I've never had anyone here before. In this house."

"Ever?"

"Ever. When the scandal hit I had to leave D.C. immediately. I stayed with my father for a time, but he quickly tired of the *situation*. And my brother and his wife felt the same way. Plus, they had young children in the house they didn't want to expose to...well, me, I guess. Anyway, I scrambled and bought this house. I needed something with a fence that would clearly delineate the property line so if any reporters crossed it I could call the police and press charges. I also needed..."

"A place to hide."

He understood. He would. "Yes. In the months following I couldn't leave at all. Something as simple as going to the grocery store was a battle. So anything I wanted I had delivered here. It was so much easier. My family wanted nothing to do with me. My friends...well, I didn't have friends as much as I did colleagues, and in political circles I was poison. So I had this house and I filled it with all the things that would comfort me and I hunkered down here."

"Didn't it make you go stir-crazy?" he asked. "Not having anyone to talk with about what was happening?"

"Not really. I didn't want to talk about it. You know what I did, my reasons behind it. How could I tell anyone that? No, I was perfectly content to be here alone. At times I even wondered if I had gotten agoraphobic, because the idea of leaving the house would send me into a small panic. But eventually things calmed down, and the reporters moved on to the next story, and I wasn't afraid to leave anymore. Still, in the last five years of working, most of it I did out of my house. Yours was the first business trip I made. I didn't want to go, but Ben made me do it."

"Thank you, Ben."

She smiled wryly. "I'm really not crazy. I mean, the scandal is behind me. I can shop now or be about town and hardly anyone recognizes me anymore. But this will be the first time anyone's actually been inside. I guess I'm a little nervous."

"What about your family? Surely they had to come around after all this time. I mean, they're family."

He said it like he expected all families to be forgiving. But hers wasn't. At least not her father, not even at the end of his life.

"When it happened, my father's health was failing. I couldn't blame him for not having the strength to deal with it. With me. It was easier, for both of us, to stay apart."

Until the end came and even Robert had to concede that a daughter should see her father for the last time. It had been a mistake. Instead of bringing him any peace in his final moments, it had only made him more agitated.

Madeleine couldn't blame the morphine or anything else, because as he thrashed on the sheets he looked right at her and called her Jezebel. In time, she was able to come to understand that he hadn't been in his right mind. His illness had taken much of his mental health as well as his physical health. Still, it hurt.

She didn't want to share that with Michael, though. It seemed silly to her, but she didn't want him to know what her father had thought about her in the end.

"And your brother?"

"After a time, Robert and I came to an... understanding. He hasn't exactly forgiven me for everything that happened. And as a very high-profile lawyer in Philadelphia, he was never going to invite me to any social events or parties he might host. But he and his wife, Gale, have had me over for the holidays a couple of times in the last few years. I think they felt a little guilty for shutting me out so completely after it happened."

"They should feel guilty. They should have supported you, not shunned you."

"You're defending me again." She smiled. "I told you not to."

"I will always defend you. As I said before, you made a mistake. It happens. Your brother should realize that and get over it."

"Maybe, but the truth is we were never really that close growing up. We were always too competitive with each other, a competition my father liked to fuel. So it's not like I felt a loss for him in particular. Maybe only family in general."

"I still want to punch him in the teeth."

"That might be fun to watch." She chuckled. "Okay, let's do this. Michael, would you like to come inside my home?"

"You sure? You're not worried you left your underwear on the floor?"

"No." She swatted his arm.

"I bet you've got glass ring stains on all your tables. Maybe dried milk at the bottom of cereal bowls left scattered throughout the house."

"Now you're being ridiculous."

"Oh, shit…you're not a hoarder, are you? I've seen those shows on TV and those houses creep me the hell out."

He was playing with her, and in an odd way it helped to calm her nerves. "You'll just have to see." She got out of the car and he followed, grabbing his overnight bag from the backseat and swinging it over his shoulder.

She unlocked the front door and swung it open. "I hope you don't mind cats. I've got twenty-three of them."

He stopped at the door.

"Kidding."

"That," he said seriously, "was not funny."

It was a little funny. Cautiously he stepped inside and she felt the tension suddenly leave her. Nothing cataclysmic had happened. Her heart didn't freeze up. This was Michael—he wasn't out to hurt her. She took his bag and left it on the stairs. Then she gave him a tour.

He looked at everything. Every piece of art she'd hung on the walls, every knickknack she'd collected over the years. He ran his hand along the throw blankets she kept on the couch in her living room, and he studied each pillow as if it were a work of art in itself.

He stopped in front of a long table in her living room that was covered with personal photos. He lifted one of her and the former president to study it.

"Really?"

"I know. Strange that I would keep it, right? But it is from the night of the election. We had just won and I was euphoric. It was a really big moment in my life. My greatest achievement. I couldn't throw it out."

"You're allowed to be proud of your accomplishments," he agreed. "Not everything has to be defined by one single moment."

After showing him the great room, the kitchen and the dining room she'd converted into her home office, she felt as if every aspect of her personality was on display.

"Well?"

Of course it didn't matter what his opinion meant. After all, it was her house and her taste and if he didn't like it, he didn't like it. It was ridiculous to feel this way, but this was her private castle. And she had finally lowered the drawbridge for him. She wanted him to like it.

He took time to consider his answer. "I think it's a reflection of you. And I think it's beautiful."

That's when she knew. In that one solitary moment. She was in love with him.

But on the heels of that revelation came the sadness of wondering if love was going to be enough to fix either of them.

CHAPTER FIFTEEN

"Are you ready for the big news?"

Later that night they were on the couch and Madeleine was pressed up against him. The television was on and some attractive redhead was telling them what the week's weather was going to be like.

She turned to him with an irritated expression. "You have news and you waited all this time to tell me?"

"You had a big day and I didn't want to overload you. You were at the hospital with Ben all morning, then letting someone into your house for the first time, letting someone eat off your kitchen plates for the first time, sit on your couch for the first time..."

She punched him in the stomach and he broke off his list with a whoosh of air.

"I get it. Now, what's the news?"

"I have a tentative deal for a partnership with Blakely."

"Blakely. He was your first choice, wasn't he?"

Michael nodded. "I like the way he runs his company. He's solid and his decision making is for the long-term."

Madeleine sat up straighter as she realized how exciting this was for him. "That's great. That's amazing."

"Turns out the automotive industry is getting pressure from the current administration to really amp up their electric-car production. Unfortunately, the demand from consumers isn't there. Blakely thinks my car can change that, and he's right. He has to appear before a congressional committee in a couple of weeks and he wants me to go with him. He believes that will satisfy the environmental concerns and at the same time will offer us a great forum to announce the future of the auto industry."

"You did it!" She beamed.

"You did it."

"No, I only arranged for you to be seen at the right places and cleaned up your bad-boy image. You did the work. And the car is going to be fantastic. As soon as it rolls off the production line, I'm buying one."

"Awesome. That's one. We only need to sell maybe a couple of million more to call it a success."

"Hey, this means you don't have to do the

interview. There's no point now. You already have what you wanted."

Michael considered that, but the marketing people had been thrilled when he'd told them about *Sunday Night Hour*. Free publicity was the best kind, after all. And tying him to the car would give it more appeal to a younger market. Who didn't want to own something a Formula One race-car driver built?

"I've already committed to doing it. I know it doesn't necessarily matter now, but I'm going to do it, anyway."

Madeleine snapped her mouth closed.

He understood her concern, but he could handle it. "I told you not to worry about me. Your friend Peg isn't going to learn anything that I don't want her to know. I've taken care of everything."

It was strange, too, but the idea of the interview wasn't nearly as intimidating now as it had been when she'd first suggested it. Maybe having dealt with Nooky so effectively made him less fearful that someone from his past was going to jump up and start telling all his secrets.

Or maybe the fact that he had finally told his secret to someone relieved its hold on him. The truth was out there. Madeleine knew what had happened to him, knew the psychological results, and it didn't matter to her. She was still pressed up against him on her couch, excited about what he'd been able to accomplish.

And she was worried for him. Because she cared about him. All good things.

"I don't want to see you put in a bad position. I don't want you to be taken by surprise or..."

He tilted her face slightly and kissed her into silence. Then, because he liked kissing her, he did more of it. When he felt her hands reach around his neck, though, he stopped. This was what had gotten them into trouble the last time.

"I think we should call it a night."

He didn't want a repeat of what had happened a week ago in the hotel. Better to put a stop to it before it got out of control. Because for reasons Michael couldn't fathom, things always got out of control with her.

That had never happened to him before. With any of the women he'd dated, he'd always stayed in his head the whole time thinking about his next move. What would he do here? How would it make her feel if he touched her there?

For him, sex was a play he needed to perform. He needed to make sure he knew his lines and all the blocking and he wanted to make sure his audience was always well entertained. Never before had he lost control, or lost himself in the moment.

But with Madeleine, he could actually forget for a time that he wasn't a whole person.

A normal man.

After he had left her that night at the hotel and had time to cool down and think about what had happened, he'd tried to see things from her perspective. It made some sense why she didn't want him to take the blue pill or simply pleasure her. It wasn't completely because she was afraid to let go sexually. After all, it would be pretty hard to let herself be that vulnerable when she knew the person she was with couldn't let go with her. That they weren't together on the same sexual plane.

He wanted to tell her that he was there with her more than he'd ever been with anyone else, even back in high school when he'd been with every girl who would let him between her legs. But he was tired of talking about sex. Tired of discussing the elephant that wasn't going to go away and was probably eventually going to tear them apart.

How could it not?

For now, he could go to bed and she could

go to bed, and tomorrow they would see Ben together, and he would offer whatever support she needed. It would be enough.

"I'll show you the upstairs," she said, moving away from him. Already he missed the warmth of her body pressed against his side.

There were three bedrooms upstairs. Hers was the master bedroom at the end of the hall. The second room housed a treadmill and some free weights.

Yeah, she would have needed a private gym during the year of the scandal. It was like she'd been imprisoned. Granted, her digs were nicer than his cell had been in prison, but the result was the same. They had both lost their freedom because they had done really stupid things.

It didn't seem right that they were both still paying for those mistakes. They had done their time in solitary. Shouldn't that have been enough?

The third room was a guest bedroom—although why she had one, he couldn't fathom.

"I guess you want to sleep in here," she said, turning on the light.

No, he didn't. He wanted to take her hand and lead them down the hallway to her bedroom, and he wanted to lay her on the bed and strip everything off her body until she was completely bare, completely open to him. Then he wanted to come inside her and forget about all the pain he carried with him. Pain he was so damn tired of carrying.

"Yeah, this works."

She leaned in and kissed his cheek. "Okay. Good night, then."

"Yeah, yeah. Good night."

He watched as she made her way down the hallway. With each step she was moving away from him, and it felt like his heart broke a little more. He wanted to be with her, not alone. And given that today she'd done the unthinkable and let him inside her fortress of solitude, he was pretty sure she didn't want to be alone, either.

"Madeleine," he said, following her. He didn't think about his decision, he just acted. When he reached her, he took her hand. "We can try again if you want."

She nodded. "I want to. We can sleep together. That's all."

Sleeping. It sounded a lot easier than it was.

An hour after they both had settled into bed, Michael was still staring at the ceiling and had decided he probably wasn't going to sleep at all that night. Which was fine. He'd gone without sleep before.

The truth was, he was actually enjoying himself. Madeleine was practically lying on top of him with one leg slung over his thighs, her arm across his stomach and her head resting against his chest. For someone who hadn't slept with a man in a very long time, she was having no trouble making herself comfortable. And if the soft sounds coming out of her mouth were any indication, she was dead-to-the-world asleep, which meant she obviously didn't feel as odd about being with him as he did with her.

Not that it was odd. Just different. They had mimicked their routine from the other night in the hotel. Since he'd brought a T-shirt, he wore that with his boxer briefs. She'd changed into her cotton shorts and T-shirt, as well. This time, they settled into bed with no kissing and no fondling, both on their backs and with the lights turned off.

He imagined that if there had been a mirror above them they both would have seen themselves eyes wide-open, staring back at each other. But while he remained awake, aware the whole time that he was in a bed with a woman who he was not having sex with—something he had absolutely no experience with—she at some point had actually fallen asleep.

Then she'd turned on her side and practically burrowed into him.

He thought this must be what married people do. Obviously they didn't have sex every night. So on nights when they didn't do it they must crawl into bed, snuggle up against each other and sleep.

Marriage. The word was foreign to him. He'd never expected to have anything to do with the institution that made a time-honored tradition out of going to bed without sex. For him that tradition seemed disingenuous. Except, in reality, it didn't feel that way.

It felt nice. Soft and comfortable. Like she was part of him. He knew she made little sighing noises in her sleep. She knew he preferred boxer briefs. They were lying together on a bed and touching and one of them was sleeping.

This is what intimacy is.

As many times as he'd had sex before, he'd never had this.

Yes, it was definitely nice. He closed his eyes and didn't worry about not sleeping. He didn't worry about what they hadn't done, or what they couldn't do. He didn't worry about how the relationship might turn out tragically. He thought about how nice it was to hold Madeleine.

Minutes later, he drifted off to sleep.

SHE WAS WARM. It was the first thought that surfaced. She felt safe and comforted in a way she couldn't remember ever feeling. Snuggling closer to the source of her comfort she could smell the flavor of...warmth.

No, warmth wasn't a smell. She could smell muskiness and heat and it was delicious. She groaned in the back of her throat. She was somewhere in the time between still dreaming of Michael and waking up to face the day.

She didn't want to wake up.

In her dream, they were together in bed, wrapped around each other, stroking each other. She could feel hands on her breasts and her nipples pebbling into hard, little points. Then her hand was moving on furred skin that was so different from hers. Hard, flat planes, sharp angles and edges. She let the hand roam until she felt it caught in another hand. Their fingers interlocking.

No, don't let it end. I want more.

She was on the verge of letting herself be pulled out of the lethargy of her sexy dream when the hand that had captured hers moved down between their bodies. She felt the dip of his flat stomach. She traveled over the tiny indent of a belly button. Then her fingers slipped inside a cotton obstacle and her hand wrapped around something iron hot and wonderfully, amazingly hard.

It was thick and smooth and so hot to the touch she almost felt compelled to let it go, except the hand holding hers wouldn't let her. Instead his hand showed her how to move on the erection, how tightly he wanted her to squeeze.

Madeleine could feel her body respond with shocking arousal and she undulated against him. Something was out of place. Something wasn't right, but she didn't want to let herself think about it.

Then he rolled his head toward her and found the lobe of her ear. He sucked it between his teeth even as he continued to use her hand to feed his pleasure.

"*Yessss,* please, Madeleine. Please. *Yesss.*"

His teeth nibbled her ear for a time, then his mouth pressed against her neck and he sucked her there. She shivered against the strange, euphoric feeling. Blinking against the early morning light, she had to admit she was awake now. That this was real.

Michael was hard and she was stroking

him. She could feel a bit of moisture on the crown of his erection.

You should take him into your mouth.

The thought startled her fully alert. She'd never done that before with a man. Never thought she wanted to. What was happening?

"Michael…did you…?"

"No," he said as he removed her hand. Then he stripped out of his briefs in one quick movement. He was rolling on top of her and using his hands to shove her cotton shorts down her legs.

Then his hands were sliding back up her shirt until he was cupping her breasts. He'd cupped them before, in her dream, and it was as if they remembered his hands and responded by arching up into them.

"Are you…? Are we…?"

"Shh, don't talk. Don't say anything."

His legs wedged between her thighs and she willingly opened them. She could feel one hand leave her breasts and slide down her body until she felt fingers at the edge of where she was waiting to be touched.

"You're wet."

"I was dreaming of you."

In that moment he shifted himself and in one of the most surreal moments of her life she felt him slide deep inside her body. It wasn't so much of a thrust as it was a fitting together of two pieces. They pushed against each other and she could feel the swelling of his penis deep inside in a way she'd never felt it before.

Because you never let yourself really feel this before.

It was true. Sex for her had been an act to be accomplished. Madeleine didn't know what this was. But it was okay because it was Michael and she was safe with him.

And he was safe with her.

He lifted himself onto his arms and twisted his hips to push himself even deeper, then she waited as the slow withdrawal had her holding her breath in anticipation. When he thrust back inside, she cried out.

He pushed one hand under her ass while holding himself up with the other and steadied her as he continued pounding into her body.

There was no finesse, she thought as her body shook and her breasts jiggled against each thrust. There was only urgency and need. She could feel her body contracting in on itself. She'd never had an orgasm this way, with just the thrust of a hard cock inside her, but she knew that was going to change. She was being pulled into a vortex. And she must have started to cry because she could feel streams of wet tears sliding down her cheeks.

One hard slam and she went over the edge. Pleasure coursed through her, from her scalp to her toes, until it centered into that spot between her legs. The orgasm felt like it went on for an eternity, but then as it started to subside she heard his harsh groan over her and felt his body jerk and tighten.

She looked up expecting to see his face in ecstasy but instead saw agony. Capturing his face in her palm, she thought only to ease him as his body jerked over her and he let out a low, throaty moan.

When he collapsed, she wrapped her arms around him. It was then she realized he had been the one crying—her palms were damp from the tears he'd shed over her.

HE DIDN'T WANT to roll off her. If he rolled off her onto his back then she might roll toward him and look at him. He didn't want her to look at him. He sure as hell didn't want to talk. But he could feel her body shifting to bear his weight and he knew that wasn't fair.

Moving his hips, he slid out of her body and marveled that with such a small motion he was already starting to feel aroused again.

Flopping onto his back he covered his eyes with his forearm.

What the hell had happened?

Did this mean he was cured? Did this mean it was over? Eighteen years of mental anguish suddenly gone? Somehow he didn't think so. It would be too easy and nothing in his life had been that easy.

He would take it in stride, he told himself. He'd woken up with an early morning boner and he and his girlfriend had made love. It had been a little quick but it had been good. When she'd squeezed herself all around him, he'd felt her come.

That had been hot.

So no big deal. A typical morning with his girlfriend.

Michael rubbed his hand over his chest and tried to think about what he was feeling. But it was too much. He couldn't hold on to any one thought or any one feeling.

She was watching him. He could feel it. Scrubbing both hands over his face he could feel the dampness left by his tears and rubbed them away.

Crying…what a pussy.

He had to say something. Words immediately leaped to his lips, but he knew the statement was the stupidest damn thing to say. Still, he couldn't help it.

Rolling toward her, he could see she was still wearing her cotton T-shirt. He hadn't even managed to get that off, just slid his hands under it to cup her full breasts. He also hadn't sucked on her nipples. He wanted to do that. Wanted to pull them in his mouth and listen to her sigh his name. Next time.

Next time?

Don't think about it, he told himself. This was all for now, and it would be enough. But he had to tell her something. She was so perfect lying there with a soft smile and eyes that said she knew him too well.

"I know this is probably the absolute worst thing to say right now...but I love you."

She flinched. Probably not a good sign. Then she reached out to touch his face again. "Michael..."

He reached for her hand and caught it, then brought it to his lips and chuckled.

"I know. I know. Impotent man finally has non-chemically-enhanced sex and his first orgasm in eighteen years, he's bound to be a bit...sentimental. But I don't think it's any less true."

She was wary. He could see it in her eyes. So little trust. It made sense she wouldn't trust what he said in this moment. In this huge and miraculous moment. It made sense that she couldn't say it back because she didn't know how real his feelings were. Or if they were simply the words of a very grateful man.

He understood it, but it didn't make him happy. Madeleine Kane had to be his. She had to be.

But she had talked to him on the phone without her shoes on, and she'd invited him into her house, and more importantly, she'd gotten completely naked in bed. This morning she'd let him come inside her body.

A wise man called that progress and didn't try to push for too much.

"Okay, let's drop that topic. Can I say one more thing?"

"You can say anything you want."

It seemed silly and he considered holding his tongue but this was Madeleine.

"Thank you. You're a really great lay."

She giggled at his rough language like he knew she would. Because his Madeleine would always be shocked by his rough ways and dirty language. He wondered if she would ever admit that she liked it. Maybe next time he would talk dirty in her ear and see how she responded to that.

Next time. Yeah, it felt right. Like something had shifted inside him and this weight that had been pinning him down all these years was finally gone.

"You're welcome," she said, like a very proper lady.

CHAPTER SIXTEEN

Four weeks later

"AGAIN," MICHAEL WHISPERED into her ear as he felt the last of her orgasm subside around his still-hard cock. He wanted more for her. He wanted more for them both.

"I can't. It's too much," she groaned even as her hips rocked in time with his.

"Yes, you can." She would take everything he could give her because what if this time it was the last time? What if the memories came back and he changed back into the person he was?

Stop thinking that. You have to stop thinking that!

Michael would have loved to tell his brain exactly what to think, but unfortunately, he was finding he had little control over it. Four weeks of sex. Four weeks of Madeleine. Four weeks of feeling like a whole human being and still he wondered if this was for real.

If it would end.

If it did, then he needed to enjoy every moment of this. He needed to eat up every ounce of delicious pleasure that had been denied to him for so long. He needed her to feel how it could be between them so in case he did revert she would at least know that this was how much he wanted her.

He'd made love to her like a man obsessed with sex for the past few weeks they'd spent living here at her house. Only stopping to eat, visit Ben and take care of the most basic chores. In the beginning he wondered if she would be put off by this need. Of course she could understand why a man who hadn't reached an orgasm in the past eighteen years might be greedy. At one point he actually stopped to ask if she was doing this for him because she knew he needed it. Of course she said no.

After all, he had once accused her of not enjoying sex.

That clearly had been a mistake.

Because every time he turned to her, every time he touched her, she responded. It was like she, too, had been stuck in some kind of sexual stasis and was also enjoying the freedom of finally being released.

There were times when even he didn't think he had anything left in him that she would suddenly roll on top of him and demand that he take her.

Never once had his body failed him. Not with her.

"Michael, please," she groaned, wrapping her leg around his waist as he thrust and twisted his hips hoping to hit her in the right spot with the right amount of pressure....

There. He could feel her muscles spasm around him again, clasping him to her so hard he wondered if they might never be separated. Then it came, that delicious rush that raced down his spine and up his balls until he was coming and shuddering on top of her.

There had been times, in all those years of faking it with other women, that he'd told himself sex without an orgasm was still pleasurable. The rubbing together of bodies, the taste of a woman's breast in his mouth. Yes, once he'd tried to convince himself that coming wasn't all that important.

What a crock of shit.

"Please don't let this end," he said as he pulled away from her body, utterly and gloriously spent.

He rolled onto his back and felt her turn toward him, tucking her body around him as if they were two jigsaw-puzzle pieces coming together. It was late and they both wanted to get an early start tomorrow as the doctor was going to make his decision regarding Ben's release from the hospital. He felt no guilt at all letting himself drift into an easy sleep after making love to his woman.

"Do you think it will?"

The question brought him out of his drowsy state.

"Do I think what will?" He wasn't sure he understood the context of the question. Had he said something to her, right there at the end?

Madeleine propped her body up so she could look into his face. Although the light was out in her bedroom, the moonlight illuminated her features.

"Do you think this is going to end? Is that why we've been going at it like…like…"

"Rabbits?"

"I was going to say monkeys but rabbits works, too." He could see her frowning. He didn't want that. Not after something that had been so beautiful. "I don't want to think that this is some kind of race. Us against some ticking clock in your head. It shouldn't be like that."

"I don't know what to say. I don't know why it suddenly happened that I became whole again. And I don't know if it will stay this way." *I don't know if it will only ever work with you.* He didn't want to say that, though. That was too much pressure to lay on anyone.

"You should talk to someone again." She nudged him, then settled her head in the crook of his arm where he liked for her to be.

"It didn't work the last time."

"That's because you were looking for someone to fix you. Nobody could have done that, Michael."

"Is it important to you?"

She hesitated and he could tell she wanted him to make the decision on his own. But he'd hated talking to shrinks. Hated opening himself up. Hated handing over his secrets. So if he was going back he wanted to be able to say it was only to make her happy. Because he was coming to find out he would do anything to make her happy.

"Yes."

"Then I'll go. I'll make an appointment as soon as we get back to Detroit."

"MICHAEL, this is a surprise."

Michael shook hands with Dr. Sheffield before sitting down across from him in the oversize leather chair. There was a couch, of course, but he'd certainly never felt the need to lie down on it in all the times he'd been here before.

Dr. Sheffield looked the same as Michael remembered. Messy gray hair with an out-of-control mustache. He wore sweater-vests, which Michael didn't think modern men did anymore, and he always looked like he was happy to be exactly where he was. Which was interesting, considering the guy basically had to listen to other people's shit all day.

"When I saw your name on my schedule I was really pleased. I thought you had given up on me completely."

Michael didn't want to confess that he had. That he'd basically concluded no one could do anything for him. He figured it wouldn't be a good start to their session. But he also knew, especially with Dr. Sheffield, that lying to his therapist wasn't helpful, either. Not if he hoped to make any progress.

"I had given up. For a time. I guess, when it wasn't working, I didn't see the point."

The doctor shrugged. "Most don't. People come to see a psychologist with a lot of expectations. That I can give them answers they are looking for, that I can tell them what they are doing wrong in their lives and how to fix it. That I can cure them. You're too smart for that, I think. You always were."

Maybe not. Michael at one time had believed that seeing a doctor would make his problems go away. It only made sense. If there was something wrong with you physically a doctor should be able to fix you. If there was something wrong with you mentally then a shrink should do the same. Madeleine was right about that. His expectations had been too high.

Of all the shrinks he'd seen, he'd liked Dr. Sheffield the most. The man didn't offer any bullshit. Just his impressions and his understanding.

"So why did you come back?"

"I had an erection." Michael closed his eyes briefly, embarrassed that saying the words could still choke him up.

"Did you orgasm?"

"Yes." Michael was uncomfortable talking about this with another man. But this was a man who knew everything about him, anyway.

"That's excellent. Can you talk about it?"

Not able to stay still, Michael stood and started pacing behind the chair while the doctor sat calmly and listened.

"I met someone. A woman I care very much about. Oh, hell, I love her. I can say that to you, although she doesn't like to hear it very much."

"What's she like?"

This, Michael thought, was his favorite topic. "She's amazing. She's brilliant and strong. She's poised and elegant. But she's also warm and generous. Comforting. Like this home base I never had. I could listen to her for hours, but she's not someone who talks for the sake of hearing herself. I'm always fascinated by her. She makes me play board games, which I find ridiculous, but I play them, anyway, mostly so I can watch her get fiercely competitive. Which is a total turn-on."

"Do you mean that literally?"

Michael laughed. "Very literally. Like two times a day literally. I think she's starting to wonder what she unleashed. It is crazy. I knew when I first met her that she was different. And it wasn't easy between us and it took time. I had to tell her the truth first…"

"You told her what happened to you in prison."

"I had to. She caught me trying to take a pill and I had to tell her the truth."

"You didn't *have* to do anything," Dr. Sheffield told him. "I suspect if you go back and think about it, you'll see maybe you knew you could tell her. Or maybe you'll find you even wanted to tell her."

"No way. I would never have wanted to tell her that. It's too ugly. But it was either the truth or risk losing her. I couldn't let that happen."

Slowly the doctor nodded. "So she became more important than your secret."

Yes. Michael could see that clearly.

"And when that happened," Sheffield continued, "your secret became less important to you. You could start to put the events of your past in perspective."

"You're saying telling her the truth cured me."

"Cured is a strong word. Yes, you can get an erection now. Have sex now. But you still decided to come back and see me."

He was about to say Madeleine had told him to, but he stopped. The truth was he didn't mind being back here. As much as he hated opening himself up like this, he knew this was a good thing. Or maybe he was hoping to find a second opinion to confirm he was indeed fixed. "I guess I wanted to figure out why now. Why with her?"

"I can tell you from listening to you talk about her that your feelings for her seem very real. You chose to tell her your secret, so you trust her. That, combined with what I imagine is a strong sexual attraction to this woman, helped you overcome the trauma of your past."

"You make it sound easy. Like I could have done this all along."

"Maybe you could have."

"But I didn't. Not until I fell in love. And I have to tell you, the idea that love saved me seems really lame here."

"No. Love is a wonderful and very powerful emotion, but I would never say that someone else was responsible for what you accomplished. You fixed you, Michael. You figured out how to open yourself to someone. You decided to trust this person. You found a way to let go of the past and its hold on you. You did that."

Michael stopped moving and realized how good those words made him feel. It wasn't just Madeleine who healed him. Which meant even if he lost her, he wouldn't go back to life as it was before.

Because he had to face the reality that he still might lose her. After weeks of standing by her side while she was there for Ben, after weeks of living together in her house and sharing a life with her, after weeks of making love to her freely, she still hadn't said she loved him.

Michael sat again in the leather chair, his elbows on his knees with his hands interlocked. "I think I was afraid if I lost her…it would all go away."

"And you're worried about losing her."

"Yeah." He sighed, leaning back in the chair. This was good, he thought. He needed to talk about this with someone. "I guess you could say she has issues."

"Most people do. In one form or another."

Madeleine would be angry with him for doing this. But the man wasn't a reporter or someone who would ever violate the confidentiality of a therapy session.

"She's Madeleine Kane."

"Madeleine… Why do I know that name? Is she an actress…? Oh. Wait. *That* Madeleine Kane?"

"Yep." The doctor said nothing and Michael continued. "I'm having a hard time getting her to trust me. I can see it happening in bits and pieces but she's not all the way there."

"You want it to happen faster."

"I want her. Period. Like, yesterday."

"I would tread carefully, Michael. Given what I know of her past, which really isn't any more than the media reported, I would imagine she would have to be cautious with any relationship."

"Cautious doesn't even begin to cover it."

"If she's opening up to you, let her continue to do so at her pace. She'll need to feel comfortable. I would also imagine she'll need to feel very, very safe."

"There is nothing to be afraid of anymore. I keep trying to tell her that. All that stuff she went through is over."

"Over in your opinion. But maybe not over for her. Just as for so long what happened in prison wasn't over for you."

Michael nodded. "Slow and steady…"

"Wins the race. Or possibly the girl, in this case." The older man smiled as he spoke.

Michael stood and offered his hand to the doctor. "Thanks for this. This was good."

"You'll come back?"

"Do I need to?"

"Only if you want to, Michael."

"Okay. Thanks. I didn't really have anyone I could talk to about her. She'll barely be seen with me in public. I mean it when I say she has issues. She's got *issues*."

"Of course she does," the doctor said. "She was willing to pursue a relationship with an impotent man. That tells me a lot."

Michael tried not to be bothered by that statement, but all the way home he wondered which version of himself Madeleine felt safer with.

"I DIDN'T wake you?" Ben asked over the phone.

"No," Madeleine lied. "Of course not." Because lying around in bed with her lover until the late morning was entirely too indulgent.

In truth, the ringing phone had woken them both, but she couldn't be mad when it was Ben calling. At his command they had left Philadelphia last week, as his condition continued to improve daily. He'd already been released from the hospital several days early with the stipulation he remain at home for another two weeks of strict quarantine. But so far all signs were good.

The cancer was gone. And no signs of rejecting the bone marrow. He was still weak and exhausted a lot of the time, but the doctors said over time he would get his strength back.

"I was curious about when the interview is happening. You hadn't said when you were here."

"Actually, Peg is coming out this afternoon with a film crew to get started. She says it should take a few days to get all the footage she wants," Madeleine said into her cell. Peg had called last week to set up the schedule. A few days of shooting and the interview would air in two weeks.

"He's ready for it?" Ben asked.

Madeleine watched as Michael pulled back the covers of the bed and walked shamelessly naked across the room to the bathroom. The sight of his narrow hips and tight buttocks was something she would never grow tired of seeing.

They'd lived in his house since their return to Detroit, and even though it had only been weeks between living at her house and now living at his, it felt like they'd always had this life. As if they had always spent their days together when he wasn't needed at the office and their nights cooking and watching TV when he got home. As if they had always gone to bed together and made love together and woken up ready to do it all over again.

"He's as ready as he can be. I hope I've covered every avenue Peg might explore."

"I'm sure you have. So...what happens next? When the interview is done will you continue your...vacation?"

Madeleine didn't pretend not to know what Ben's question meant. She had told him about their relationship. He had seen them together as a couple when they were sitting outside his quarantined room. They had talked with him every day for weeks. And while they didn't hold hands or make out in front of him, anybody in the world could look at them and know they were lovers.

He knew it was obvious when they looked at each other. When they made an effort not to kiss each other or hold hands. So when Ben asked what was next, what he was really asking was if she was coming back to Philadelphia. Ever.

"I don't know. I think…" She gulped. "I think if he lets me, I would stay here…for a while."

"Lets you?"

Right. Bad choice of words. It implied she was begging for him to let her stay. But, in truth, she needed to stay. Because she needed him.

All of those things were so dangerous. So scary.

"Wants me to. And if I decide I want to. Or would like to. Maybe. Or I could decide to leave. I don't know…"

Her babbling was cut off by a rumbling chuckle from the other side of the phone. She was happy to know she at least made him laugh.

"Ben, stop asking me questions I don't know the answer to. You know I hate that."

"Okay. Keep me up-to-date."

"I will. And how is the nurse working out?"

"She's fine," he said, his tone clipped. "I think I can let her go, actually. I'm feeling stronger every day and can finally take care of myself."

"Don't push it, Ben. You know you're not out of the woods yet."

"Yet. But I will be soon. I can sense it. I feel whole again. Like the thing that was eating me up from the inside is finally gone for good."

"That's great. Just don't overdo it."

"You sound like Anna."

Madeleine waited. In all the time she and Michael had sat with him keeping him company he'd never once mentioned Anna. Had never even said her name. Or asked where she might have gone. Madeleine thought that was revealing in its own way.

She knew what Anna thought he felt about their time together and she knew what Anna had told her he'd said. But sometimes what a person said wasn't always what they meant.

Or what a person didn't say wasn't always how they felt.

Madeleine had personal experience with this.

"Do you want to talk about it?" she asked tentatively.

"No."

She figured as much. "I have her new cell number. She gave it to me."

"That she felt she needed to change the old one was ridiculous and immature. What did she think…I was going to harass her? Stalk her? She quit. End of story. I have no intention of contacting her."

But somehow, he knew her previous number was no longer in service. Madeleine debated telling Ben her thoughts. She didn't want to be disloyal to Anna, but if there was any hint of feeling for his former assistant, he needed to know where Anna was coming from. "I think she did it more for herself than out of spite for you."

"Explain."

"I don't think she wanted to know you weren't trying to contact her. Sometimes a phone that doesn't ring is the hardest sound to listen to."

There was silence. Madeleine waited patiently, wondering if he would ask for the number she'd offered. Not that he needed to get it from her. If Ben wanted to track down Anna, he would.

"I should go."

"Of course," Madeleine said, backing off. She'd given him enough to think about it. "I'll let you know my schedule as soon as I can."

"Goodbye."

Madeleine ended the call just as Michael was coming back into the bedroom fresh from his shower. A towel was wrapped low around his hips and she could see beads of water still clinging to his body.

She wanted to lick each one of them off.

Ducking her head to hide her blush, she marveled at her sexual attraction to this man. Everything he did got to her. He once burped in front of her and while she'd scolded him, it also made her consider what a man he was. Following on the heels of that thought was an intense desire.

After he'd burped.

She was…besotted. There was no other word for it.

No, there was another one; she just wouldn't let herself use it. Couldn't let herself use it until she knew for sure that his feelings were more substantial than something born from gratitude.

Instinctively she held the sheet up over her breasts and watched as the motion drew his attention to her body. She shifted under his scrutiny, but when she looked at him, he was tossing the towel and revealing the front view.... It was more fun than the back view.

"Well, that is impressive." She smiled.

He looked down at himself and caught his hardening penis in his hand. His smile was almost as big as his erection. "I know." He looked at her and wiggled his eyebrows.

She'd never had this much fun with men and sex. But before she got lost in it again, she did have questions.

Michael took two steps and essentially fell onto the bed on top of her. His mouth aimed for her neck and he kissed her there, knowing it drove her wild. She moved her head to kiss him and he shook his head.

"No, you can't. I've already brushed my teeth and you haven't brushed yours."

"You're saying a little morning breath is going to stop you from putting your tongue in my mouth?"

"Yep. We're not on equal ground. Two morning breaths cancel each other out. But when one has brushed and the other hasn't...

ewww. So we're going to have to do this sans mouth kissing. Let's try it this way to avoid any temptation."

He rolled onto his back and tugged the sheet away from her. With effortless strength he pulled her on top of him so that his erection was bumping against her bottom and his hands were kneading her breasts.

"What makes you think I want to do it at all?" she asked, slightly miffed.

He let one hand slide down the middle of her body until a knuckle was pushing through the folds between her legs, making her squirm on top of him and rub her butt against his penis. "That."

"You're shameless."

"I'm horny. And happy to be so."

She looked down at him and her breath almost caught. He *was* happy. She could see it in his face. The lines around his eyes seemed to have eased and the tension she had always associated with him was gone.

"You never did tell me what Dr. Sheffield said."

. He stopped plucking her nipples, and she was slightly disappointed, but she couldn't help her curiosity. She knew he'd made an appointment to see a therapist he liked. When he'd gotten back from the appointment last night and she had asked him about it, he'd simply said he was cured and then started kissing her. Which made her forget everything else.

But cures for psychological trauma didn't easily happen and they both knew it.

His hands dropped to her hips and he held her in place on top of him.

"We talked. It was good. He basically said I had been ready to let go and I did. So now I'm fixed. Yay me."

She brushed her fingers over his chin. "I think you always have it in you to do whatever you set your mind to."

Again Michael's eyes twinkled. "Really? Well, right now I'm setting my mind to getting inside you and making you come really hard. Then I'm taking you out for brunch afterward. How's that for goals?"

"Michael." She chastised his crude language ever so slightly. She would never admit it to him, but secretly it thrilled her.

Then he went ahead and did exactly what he said he was going to do, just like he always did.

CHAPTER SEVENTEEN

"WE'RE GOING." Michael already had his coat on and was standing in the foyer with his car keys in his hand.

"Why can't we make breakfast here?"

"Because I want to go out with you. And not to some dark movie theater. I want to be in the sunlight with you in public. It's a gorgeous spring morning. We've got nowhere in particular to be for several hours. Let's go get breakfast and drink mimosas."

"You can't be drinking. Peg and her crew are coming today. You need to be sharp and completely on your game."

"Fine. I'll stick to orange juice." He frowned at her. "It's time you get over this, Madeleine."

Get over it, she thought. Easier said than done. "Why suddenly now? We've been together for weeks and this hasn't been an issue. You've been fine with the way things are. At least I thought you were."

"I am fine. More than fine. I'm the happiest I've ever been. But what are we doing here if not starting a life? This is where I live. I want to show you the places I like to go, take you to all the places where I like to hang out. Heck, I would like to introduce you to my neighbors."

The neighbors. How could she possibly do that?

Oh, hi, I'm Madeleine Kane, Michael Langdon's girlfriend. Remember me? That's right. I'm the scandalous whore and home wrecker, but we should all get together at the block party and share stories.

"I told you how I felt about this. If we can get past the interview, let any attention that might come out of that die down for a time, then maybe in a couple of months—"

"A couple of months?" Michael sputtered. "Are you kidding me? Madeleine, this is it, we're together now and I'm tired of hiding."

"You're not the one who has to hide."

"You don't have to hide, either."

She shook her head. "You don't know how it will be. You said it—this is your hometown. Someone might see you and wonder who you are with. People know you date celebrities so they will look at me a little more closely. And then it will be the same old thing. 'Why does she look so familiar? How do I know her…? Oh, that's right. She's the president's girl.'"

She watched his jaw clench and knew he hated it when she talked about herself like that, but it was the reality of how other people thought of her.

"I know it's hard. I *know* it's hard. But you can't spend the rest of your life wondering when the past will catch up with you. We're a couple and when I go out I want you with me. So put your coat on, get in the car and come eat some damn waffles with me."

Madeleine bristled. "That sounds suspiciously like a command."

He approached her carefully and probably with good reason because she had an overwhelming urge to run. Back upstairs to the bedroom or even all the way home to Philadelphia.

Michael softened his tone. "Look, I know it's scary. But you do realize your fears are groundless. You don't know that anyone will see us. And if someone did what's the worst that could happen?"

They would stare at her. And the whole time they were staring at her, she would know what they were thinking.

Slut. Whore.

One mistake. She'd made one damn mistake. Tears came to her eyes and Michael hissed.

"No, no. Please don't do this. It's just brunch. If you don't want waffles you can have whatever you want. French toast, oatmeal…"

She knew he was trying to tease her, but it didn't loosen the knot in her stomach. "Michael, I know you think my fears are silly…"

"Not silly. I get it. You were hunted by the media. If I could go back in time and change everything they did to you, and rewrite everything they said about you and make it all go away, I would."

"But you can't."

"Nope. I figured out a long time ago that there is nothing to be done about changing the past. But this is now. You and me. We need to be able to live our lives normally."

"Yes," she said, clinging to his words. "Now! On the day you are being filmed. The day of your big announcement. Let's not forget Blakely hasn't signed anything with you. What if word gets out about who you are seeing and he doesn't like the idea of us or the thought of negative press? I'm doing this for your own good."

He shook his head, calling her on what she knew was a lie.

"No, you're not. You're doing this because you're still afraid. It's why you hid in your house for all those years. It's why you still put up walls to keep me out."

"I don't have walls..." she argued but stopped when he pressed a finger to her lips.

"You do. Plenty of them. And I will break all of them down, I swear it. One damn brick at a time if I have to. If you're ever going to believe I love you, if you are ever going to trust me enough to love me back, we need to get over everything we've been afraid of. I'm working on my end.... I need you to work for it, too. Take that first step. Come outside with me. Please."

He reached his hand out to her and her first instinct was to take it. It was when her brain kicked in and began to think too much that she tightened up. When she retreated behind her walls. Because he was right. She did have them.

But she didn't want them anymore. They were keeping her from him. She was keeping herself from him, and if she was ever going to have a chance at happiness, real happiness, she knew this was it.

He was it.

Michael was right. She needed to take this step forward. For him.

"Okay."

He smiled. "That's my girl."

"But I don't like oatmeal. I prefer eggs."

"Eggs it is."

"Now for your next step."

They were eating brunch at a table for two near the window that overlooked a main street in downtown Grosse Pointe. When they had been seated, he could see Madeleine was stiff, but after a cup of coffee and some pleasantries with the waitress, and when no one had pointed at her or shouted "Jezebel," she had started to relax.

Looking at her now as she moaned a little bit over her bite of eggs Benedict, he thought she might actually be glad she'd come here. Glad to sit here with him and be his date. But this step she'd taken to come out with him was really only the first of many.

He thought about what Dr. Sheffield had said about taking it slow. It was good advice, and made total sense, but Michael was fighting every instinct he had to do it.

Michael drove fast, moved fast and wanted everything with Madeleine…fast.

Like a general he needed to lay out his strategy for moving forward. Because they were moving forward. The other option, the one in which he might not be able to hold on to her, he dismissed. He simply wouldn't let it happen.

No, Michael was sure she didn't realize it yet, but Madeleine was soon going to be Mrs. Michael Langdon. He wouldn't have it any other way. It was difficult to admit, because the realization scared the crap out of him, but he needed her.

Like air and food and water.

Yeah, it was scary to know how much she meant to him. But it was also a little thrilling. Like he was in this race and marriage was the finish line, and he knew he had what it took to get there. He only needed to execute the plan.

She swallowed her bite of eggs and chased it with some coffee. "What next step? I'm here, aren't I? Without my sunglasses."

"Yes, we've now conquered your fear of daylight. See, it's not so bad."

"I suppose I haven't started to melt." She smiled.

"So we proceed to our next step. I told you Blakely and I are going to D.C. to speak before a congressional committee about the impact of the electric car. Both on the environment and the auto industry as a whole."

"Yes."

He took a deep breath. This was a risk, but when the idea came to him he thought it sounded so right. What better way to get over the worst of her fears than by going back to the place it first happened and confronting the memories head-on?

"I want you to come with me."

She laughed.

"I'm not joking."

Her smile fell and instantly he knew he'd screwed up. "Yes, you are. Because even suggesting such a thing would be nothing more than cruel, so you must be joking."

Michael knew she wouldn't take his idea easily, but he wasn't prepared for the pain he saw in her eyes. He'd caused that pain and it killed him. "I'm not trying to be cruel. I'm trying to help you overcome your fear."

"I get it," she said tightly, throwing her napkin on the table. "I see what this is all about now. You're cured. All better. Congratulations. Now poof, I'm supposed to let go of everything, too, and join you in happy land where the past doesn't hurt us anymore."

It sounded silly to hear her say it, but yes, he supposed that was what he thought might happen. She'd helped him. He wanted to help her. It only seemed right. Like they were rock climbers using each other to work their way up the cliff. She was his safety first while he made his move upward. Now it was his turn to make it okay for her to come up behind him.

"Well, maybe I'm not you. In fact, I know I'm not you because I can't do it. I can't forget what happened. I can't make it go away. I was humiliated. I was decimated. I was literally spit on by people in that city and you think I would ever go back? How could you even suggest it?"

Michael closed his eyes at the sound of anguish in her voice. He didn't want to hurt her, but he had to get through to her. "I think you have nothing to be ashamed of—"

"I have *everything* to be ashamed of!"

Some of the customers at the tables around them turned their heads at her raised voice. He could see them looking over at her, and watched as she practically shrunk in on herself, turning her face away from all of them.

Away from him.

This couldn't be his Madeleine. Not the brilliant strategist or the woman who fought to the death over Monopoly or could bring him low with one raised eyebrow.

This woman was cowering.

"You made a mistake," Michael said,

reaching across the table and taking her hand before she could pull it away. He forced her to look at him. Willed her to fight back against what she was feeling. "You think you're the only one in politics who ever did that? You think you're the only one who ever slept with someone they shouldn't have? You have a talent, Madeleine. A brain like nothing I've ever seen before."

"I don't need to go back to D.C. to use it," she said dully. "It works fine here and in Philadelphia."

"What if I said I need you there?" It was a bold move on his part. Because if she told him that didn't matter to her, then he might have to realize *he* didn't matter to her. At least not enough.

"No," she said. "This isn't about you or your car or the committee. You said it. This is the next step. This is some milestone you think I need to reach before I can be ready for you, and I'm telling you that's not the case. What I feel for you isn't going to change because of this. I promise you that. But hear this very clearly, nothing…*no one*…can ever make me go back there."

"Madeleine…" Michael's phone buzzed in his pocket, interrupting him. Normally he would have ignored it, but on the off-chance it was Blakely calling with news, he didn't want to dismiss it outright. "Hold on. This argument isn't over."

"Wrong. This argument is completely over," she said tightly.

Michael glanced at the phone and saw Archie's name. "Give me a minute, all right? It's Archie and he never calls."

Madeleine said nothing and turned her face to the window.

"Hey, Archie, what's the matter?"

"Mickey, I wouldn't call, you know that, right, but I think there might be trouble. I think I might have said something wrong."

"Talk to me."

"It's my new guy. You know, Nooky."

The name sent a shudder through Michael. With everything happening, he hadn't thought to follow up to make sure the man had left as instructed. It had been weeks since the marathon. The little shit should have been long gone by now.

"What about him?"

"Well, he took off. Haven't seen him in a couple of days."

Which could mean Michael's problem was solved. "So he took off. It happens to you. You know that. You can't save them all, Archie."

"Yeah, but now this guy called and I think... oh, shoot, Mickey, I don't know how to say this, but I told Nooky about you and Maddy. I didn't think anything of it. Just bragging, you know how I do about you. Saying how lucky you are to get such a nice girl and all. But then he puts it together, you know, about her and the president..."

"So?" Michael snapped, not really understanding where Archie was going with this.

"I got a call this morning from some guy."

"What guy? What are you talking about?"

Madeleine turned to him then, her face disapproving. She was obviously not happy with the tone he was taking with his friend. Leave it to her to defend Archie in this situation.

"He said he was a journalist or something. I didn't buy that. But he says Nooky talked to him about maybe getting paid for some pictures. The man wanted to know about you and Maddy. Where you liked to hang out and stuff. I didn't tell him nothing. But he knows where you live. He said it wouldn't be hard to find you there. Anyway, I hung up. But I didn't like him...you know what I mean.

He said some bad things about Maddy and I didn't like that, either."

"Okay, Archie. Thanks for telling me."

"We're still okay, kid?"

"Yeah, yeah, we're good. I'll talk to you soon."

Michael ended the call and sat slowly back in his chair, his mind racing with possibilities. Nooky knew about him and Madeleine. He knew who Madeleine was and now someone claiming to be a journalist was interested in pictures. Pictures of him and Madeleine together.

This wasn't happening. It couldn't be. He should have paid the weasel off. Instead Nooky had found another way to make a buck.

Damn it! His past was coming back to hurt her. It was untenable. It was his worst nightmare come true.

No, it was *her* worst nightmare coming true.

Michael reached across the table and grabbed her hand. Grosse Pointe wasn't a big town and anybody asking where Michael Langdon liked to hang out on Sunday mornings might easily be led to this place. He needed to get her back to his house. Fast.

"Madeleine, listen to me. We need to leave."

"Agreed," she said, obviously still angry with him.

It happened so quickly. A flash, a blink. He could almost imagine he was hearing the sound, the soft *click-click* of a camera. But his brain couldn't catch up with the fact that this was actually happening.

Not until he saw the look of horror on Madeleine's face as she stared out the window of the restaurant.

There, on the sidewalk, was a man with a camera that had a zoom lens snapping shot after shot of them. He was actually waving at them as if they might pose for him.

Instantly Michael was on his feet. The abruptness of the movement toppled his chair and in seconds he was outside chasing down the cameraman, who quickly figured out the couple was not happy about having their picture taken. He'd almost caught up to him, but then the guy hopped into the backseat of a cab that appeared to be waiting for him.

As they sped away, Michael considered getting in his car and giving them a chase, but as soon as the cab took the first turn he knew it was hopeless.

It didn't matter how fast he could drive

if he didn't know where the other car was going.

"Damn it!" Michael shouted to an empty street. But he couldn't deal with that now. He had more important damage control to do.

When he entered the restaurant, he apologized to the rattled hostess. At the table, Madeleine was signing the credit-card slip and handing the check back to the waitress.

Her hands were shaking.

"Madeleine…"

"Please don't say anything. Just get me out of here."

Having made enough of a spectacle, he decided it was better for them to be alone. He escorted her back to his car, but found that as soon as they were alone together he didn't have a clue what to say.

"I'm sorry." It seemed the best place to start.

"It's not your fault."

"I wish I could say it wasn't. This guy, Nooky, is an ex-con I did time with. I don't know if you remember Archie talking about him. It was his new project down at the shop." Michael took a deep breath. "He was the guy from the park that day at the marathon."

"Why would he track you down at the park?"

"He was trying to shake me down for some money. He knew what I'd done to Ricca and thought I might be worried if that got out. He was blackmailing me, but I told him to get lost. Obviously, not successfully. I should have paid him. I don't know why I didn't. That's why Archie was calling me. He was trying to warn me. God, I'm sorry, Madeleine."

"You should have told me."

"I didn't tell you about him because I didn't want you to have anything to do with that garbage. I thought I was doing the right thing by standing up to him. I could have spared us all of this. Could have spared you."

"It doesn't matter," she said tightly.

"It does matter. I know you're upset. Look, I'll go land on Nooky like a ton of bricks. He'll give me the name of the photographer. Then all I have to do is buy the pictures back."

She choked out a sound. "You can't get the pictures back. They're already sold. Trust me. I have a little experience with this. My brother is probably going to see it. He's going to think it's starting again."

"Your brother? You mean the one who wasn't there for you when you needed him? Screw your brother."

"You don't understand."

No, he didn't. He didn't get why any of this was so damn important to her. Michael wanted to slam his fist through the steering wheel. This wasn't happening. Not when they were making progress. Or were they really making progress? He didn't know if he would ever get over the way her face looked after he'd asked her to come with him to D.C.

Still, he had to try to offer her something. "Okay, let's look at it this way. What happened was your worst nightmare, but how bad can it be? They got a picture of us together. We weren't doing anything illicit. We were having brunch. It shows up in a few gossip rags as some B-line story and then it's gone. That's the end of it."

"Or the beginning."

"You don't know that. For all you know, it was one and done. Hell, the picture might not even sell. You're an old scandal nobody cares about anymore."

He could see her physically react to his words.

Michael winced. "Babe, I'm sorry. I didn't mean that the way it sounded. I only meant…"

She didn't respond and he had no other words to offer. He pulled into the garage of his home and without a word she shot out of the car. Once inside she immediately headed upstairs to their room. He thought about breaking something as a way to release his fury but nothing was going to change what had happened.

Time. She needed time. Time to think and calm down. Time to put what had happened in perspective. He would give her some space. While he didn't have a lot of experience in the boyfriend role, he was fairly certain it was the sensible approach when dealing with one very pissed-off female.

Michael looked at his watch. They had a couple of hours still until Peg showed up with the crew to start filming. By then they both would have recovered their equilibrium. Everything was going to be okay, he thought as he paced back and forth in his living room.

It had to be okay.

It wasn't until twenty minutes later when she came downstairs carrying her suitcase and he was still pacing that he started to feel like maybe space and time had been the absolute wrong things to give her.

He thought the words before she said them. Thought them in his head because they were the words he was most afraid of hearing.

"I'm leaving."

It was as if someone had given him an electric jolt to the chest. Panic started to threaten at the edges but he shut it down. He needed to be calm and rational because she obviously wasn't.

"I've already booked my flight home. I've called a cab to pick me up here. I'll be gone before Peg gets here, and if I were you I would make sure any signs of my living here for the past week have been completely erased."

Completely erased. Having her here in his home, in his bed, made this the best week of his life, and she wanted to completely erase it.

"The picture will probably come out before the interview. If anything, it might generate more interest in you, which should help the ratings. But after that you'll want to quickly distance yourself from me. Any questions can be answered with minimal details. I was working for you on a consulting basis. We were having a meal together to say good-bye and end our association. Unfortunately, I don't know what the picture will actually look like. I believe you were holding my hand at the time, but who knows what he caught.

It might look as if you were reaching for the bread dish. Anything can be explained away."

"You've worked all this out in twenty minutes?" It felt like ice water was flowing throughout his body, numbing him from the inside. Did it feel the same way for her?

"Worked it out and packed. I'm efficient."

"Why are you doing this? Because you're mad at me. You blame me because of Nooky. I'm sorry I didn't tell you about him. I really didn't imagine he could come up with something like this."

She closed her eyes as if in some type of despair. "I'm not mad at you, Michael. I just can't do this. I thought I could, but I can't. I know you think it's because I can't trust you, but it's not. I trust you more than I've ever trusted anyone, but I can't do this with you. I want to go home. And it's not about the stupid picture. It's you and what you want me to be. I'm not that person. So I can't…"

"Can't what? I want to hear you say it." Maybe if she said it and he actually believed it, he would accept it and move on with his life.

"Can't be with you," she whispered.

"With me? You mean *love me.* Because if you loved me, there wouldn't be anything you couldn't do, right? I mean, if you loved me you would do whatever it took to be with me. You would be strong enough to overcome any fear or fight off any lingering guilt you have because of some stupid thing you did seven years ago."

"No, Michael, what I feel for you is so strong, but I'm not capable of doing what you ask. I can't let go of the past."

"Because you don't love me. Not enough. Say it. Please. I think I need to hear you say those words."

He watched her open her mouth, that mouth he'd kissed so many times. He waited for her to end it between them with one clean cut.

"I'm sorry," she said instead. "I'm sorry I couldn't be a better person for you. You knew about me all this time...but I didn't. I didn't know until this very moment how broken I am."

"Broken things get fixed. All the time. Look at me."

Her mouth trembled and he waited. Waited for her to say she would at least try. But a horn blared outside and that had her turning her head to the door.

"I'm sorry" was all she said.

"Me, too. Go back into hiding, Madeleine. I guess that's really where you want to be."

She didn't say anything. Simply took her bags and left, shutting the door behind her. He wasn't sure how long he stood there and looked at the closed door; he only knew she hadn't done the one thing he'd asked.

She hadn't told him that she did not love him.

CHAPTER EIGHTEEN

MICHAEL WALKED INTO Archie's shop to find Archie working alone. The old man was doing paperwork in his office while the two cars he'd prepped for oil changes sat untouched.

Michael couldn't say if he was relieved or disappointed. While he knew it was improbable Nooky would come back, Michael would have liked the chance to confront him directly. Most likely, he would have pummeled the rat, but beating people up wasn't something he did anymore.

Still, the ex-con had cost him everything. And if that wasn't worth a fist in the face Michael wasn't sure what was.

"Hey, Mickey," Archie said, coming out of his office. "So what happened? Nothing, right? Tell me that guy didn't find you. I'm so mad. I mean, what kind of crummy thing is that? I go out of my way to help an ex-con get back on his feet and he does this."

"It's pretty crummy," Michael said, not

bothering to tell Archie the photographer had found them. It would only upset him and there was no point. It wasn't Archie's fault Madeleine had left him. Hell, it wasn't even Nooky's.

Michael walked to where the worn overalls hung on the wall. He was fairly certain they were still the same ones he used to wear when he worked here. Maybe he could get Archie some new overalls. The old man would have to accept them, wouldn't he?

"What are you doing?" Archie asked.

"What does it look like I'm doing?" Michael asked as he stepped into one leg. "I'm going to help you with what you got lined up."

"You can't do that. You're a big shot now. Big shots don't change oil."

"This big shot does. Besides, you're shorthanded." Because of him. Because he wouldn't give Nooky what he wanted. If he had, maybe Madeleine would still be with him.

Don't think about her. It hurts too much.

"Hey, what's the matter with you?"

Michael zipped up his overalls and found a clean rag that he tucked into the pocket. "Nothing." Everything.

"It's not nothing. I can tell. Talk to me. What is it? Maybe Maddy wasn't happy about the picture guy knowing about you two. I hope she isn't mad at me, you know. I really like that girl for you."

"Madeleine's not my girl, Archie. In fact, she's gone. Back to Philadelphia. Things… weren't working out. Nobody's fault."

It helped to say the words. It reminded him of the reality of the situation. She was gone. She wasn't coming back. Eventually he would get over it.

Right? This hollow, empty pain wouldn't last forever, would it?

Sure, he'd heard the songs, read the stories and seen the movies. He understood conceptually that it wasn't fun when love ended. But having never been in love before, he wasn't prepared for this. The grief was stunning.

"Oh, no, you can't let her go."

"I didn't have a choice, Archie. She left and I couldn't stop her."

"Then you gotta go get her back. Right now."

Michael could see the old man was agitated, probably because he blamed himself. But it was too late. "Archie, it's done. It's over."

"It can't be over. Not yet. Maybe you had a fight and now you say you're sorry. Then you bring her some flowers. Girls like flowers."

Irritated that Archie was making it worse, Michael snapped, "What do you know about it?"

"I know you were happy with her! Really happy. I saw it when you were with her. She's the one. And you don't get something like that every day."

That was an understatement. He was thirty-seven years old and he had just experienced love for the first time. And as much as the logical side of his brain told him he might find it again someday—especially now that he was normal—he just couldn't see it.

"She left me, Archie. I can't go after her and drag her back by her hair. If she wants me, then she has to come back on her own."

"Then you need to give her a reason to come back. You need to prove to her how much you love her, because you do love her. I know it. It made me really proud. It's why I was running my mouth in the first place. All this time after prison and you were finally ready to move on with your life."

Michael balked at the idea. "What are you talking about? I moved on with my life. I became famous, hell, I became rich."

"Famous and rich didn't make you smile like she made you smile. And that's what I wanted for you."

Michael looked at the old man. He had never told Archie what had happened to him in prison, but the old man must have known there was always a lingering pain there. Something Michael had never been able to shake until he met Madeleine.

"I don't know what to do." That was the truth and it made him feel helpless. Impotent in a profoundly different way.

"You'll figure something out. You're a smart guy. All you need is a big gesture."

A big gesture. Something that would show Madeleine how much he loved her and make her come back to him. Michael thought about the television crew that was coming back to his place later this afternoon. Yesterday, he'd taken them out to his Pimp Garage to show off the car and explain the various features. Blakely had been there and he'd been asked a few questions about their partnership.

Today they were coming back to interview him exclusively. One-on-one with TV journalist Lynn Connelly.

Of course, he had an idea of what he would say and a general sense of what questions would be asked. Could he find a way to work in a big gesture during the interview? Maybe he should get down on his knees in front of the camera and beg her to come back.

He didn't imagine Madeleine would appreciate that kind of gesture. Too much attention.

Still, maybe all hope wasn't lost.

"All right, I'll think about it. In the meantime let's get these cars done."

Archie nodded. "You got it, kid. Hey, you and me working on cars together. Like old times."

Yeah, Michael thought. Like old times. And for the first time when looking back at his life he could see those old times weren't *all* bad times. He had Madeleine to thank for that realization.

A BUZZ AT the gate rang out and the sound startled Madeleine. She'd only been home for a few days and the sound was the first disturbance she'd had. And no one ever buzzed her gate. Because no one ever visited her here. Only Michael had…

Michael!

Getting up from her office, where she'd been mildly pretending to work, she ran to the foyer near the front door and hit the button that opened the gate.

She didn't bother to ask who it was because a strong part of her didn't want to be disappointed if it wasn't Michael's voice she heard through the intercom.

He'd come for her. He'd decided he was miserable without her and he would ask her to come back with him.

Which you can't do. You left him for a reason, remember?

The reality of the situation hit her like a ton of bricks. She'd left him. She'd told him she wasn't strong enough to be with him. Why would he ever in a million years come for her? Opening the front door, she was no longer surprised to see it wasn't Michael getting out of the small, efficient car.

Anna walked up the steps to where Madeleine was waiting by the front door.

"Wow. You look as bad as I feel," Anna said by way of greeting.

"I don't know. I feel pretty bad, too."

Anna pulled a bag out of her purse. It was a monster-size bag of peanut M&M's. "I find carrying chocolate with me wherever I go helps with the worst of the symptoms."

"Chocolate. I didn't think of that."

"Can I come in?"

Madeleine stepped back and, for the second time in as little as a month, let someone into her home. Maybe she was making progress, after all.

Anna looked around the place with the natural curiosity of someone who was fitting the pieces to the person.

"You want a drink?" Madeleine asked.

"Like tea?"

"Like straight vodka," she said, only partially kidding. When she first got back from Detroit she'd tried that approach. She'd found a bottle of Black Label scotch a client had given her as a gift and let herself get blisteringly drunk.

The next morning she'd woken with the same heartache plus a massive headache. So it wasn't worth it to repeat the experience. Still, there was always a second chance.

"Thanks, but I've found that doesn't help."

"I guess you're right. Okay, let's do tea. Will you share your M&M's?"

"With you? Of course."

The two women made their way back to the kitchen. Madeleine made them tea while Anna found a bowl for the M&M's and poured them in. They sat at Madeleine's kitchen table and shamelessly ate M after M.

"I wasn't sure if you wanted company or not," Anna said. "I heard from Greg you were back in town and working. I figured that wasn't a good thing."

Greg Chalmers was another member of the

Tyler Group. A formally trained psychologist, his skills included being able to detect when people were lying. An invaluable asset in corporate negotiations. "You were talking to Greg. Does that mean…?"

"No," Anna said, holding her hand up to stop Madeleine's hope. "I'm not coming back. I ran into him in the city. I've actually already found another job."

"Anna, have you considered talking to him? Telling him how you feel? I know what you told me he said, but you should see him. He's a wreck. I think part of that has to do with losing you."

"You're kidding yourself. If he's a wreck it's because he's coming off some pretty intense chemotherapy." She paused then and it was like the words were pulled out of her mouth. "How is he doing? Physically, I mean. Any signs of rejection?"

"He knows you tried to call the hospital."

Anna snorted. "Yeah, and that jackass had the nerve to take me off the list of people who had access to his information. I was only allowed to know his status. He knew what that would do to me."

"He said, and I quote, 'If Anna wants to know how I'm doing let her come down here and ask me herself.'"

"I didn't want to give him the satisfaction. Now, tell me…how is he?"

"No signs of rejection. The cancer appears to be in remission. He's tired and cranky when I call him, but it looks like he's starting to eat again. And truly, I think he does miss you. You can't tell me after years of friendship that it can be over like this. Without at least talking about it."

Anna sipped her tea. "I've got some… stuff…going on. Not really sure how it's going to pan out, but if it does we'll eventually need to have a conversation. But I don't believe it's going to change anything. Ben is nothing if not stubborn."

"I guess you're right. Who am I to talk about this, anyway? Look at me, sitting here, once again in my solitary house eating M&M's and feeling like crud."

"What happened?"

"I guess you know about me and Michael."

"Ben said you were taking a vacation. That's all I needed to know about you and Michael. But I also saw the picture."

The picture. Yes, as predicted it had hit most of the rag newspapers. Madeleine had seen it while in the grocery-store checkout line and had immediately abandoned her basket of food and run home.

But then she went back the next day and while it was still there, she realized no one was pointing at her. No one was looking at it, then at her. No one even seemed to realize it was there. It was a blurry picture in the corner with the headline Playboy Langdon Seeks Presidential Conquest.

All things considered, it could have been worse.

"So what happened?"

"I left him," she said. It felt like the stupidest thing in the world to say. How could she do something as completely stupid as leave a man like Michael Langdon?

"Uh, I hate to break this to you, but if you do the leaving you're not supposed to be the one who feels this bad."

"Yeah."

"So go back."

It wasn't as if Madeleine hadn't thought about it. But she didn't see how it was going to change anything. He would still want too much from her. Too much that she couldn't give because she was too damn afraid all the time.

"He deserves better."

"Seriously? You're Madeleine Kane. You don't get much better than that."

Anna's certainty made her smile, but it

also made her sad. "What if I told you the smart and confident Madeleine Kane you know is in fact a big fat fraud?"

Anna studied her for a moment. "I wouldn't believe it."

"It's true. I'm weak and cowardly. I hate being both those things, but I can't seem to find any other way to live. So I'm not worthy of Michael Langdon. He deserves someone who has more fight in her."

Anna sighed heavily. "Well, that sucks. You got any ice cream around this place?"

"Yeah, maybe we can put the M&M's in that."

"Now you're talking like a girl with a broken heart."

Two weeks later

MADELEINE SAT on her couch staring at a television that was most definitely turned off. It was airing tonight. His interview. She didn't know if she could watch it. She was torn between the heartache of seeing him, hearing him, and the heartache of not hearing him, not seeing him. The former would take a huge toll on her emotionally, while the latter already was.

To say she missed him was almost comical. She remembered after the scandal hit and how she'd missed her job and her friends and her father. All the things that had been lost to her.

But losing Michael wasn't filled with regret or sadness. It was like losing a limb.

For weeks she'd done battle with herself.

After Anna's visit, she tried every day to think of how she might change. What she might do. One morning she actually felt as if she had the strength to go back, after all, because living without him was way harder than being afraid of what might happen if she was with him. She had even gone so far as to book a ticket to Detroit for the following day. Not really sure what she was going to say, but hoping she might figure it out when she saw him again.

Then Madeleine went out to a drugstore to pick up a few items for her travel case and it happened. An older woman pulled out a copy of the magazine that still featured the picture of her and Michael. Madeleine stood behind her in the line with her face down, hoping the older woman didn't connect the person standing behind her with the woman in the photo.

She must not have, because instead, she

turned to show Madeleine the picture as if they were both in agreement.

"There's that horrible woman again. Look how brazen of her to be running around town like that with another man. After what she did to the First Lady and her family!"

Madeleine remembered mumbling something about having forgotten toothpaste and once again left the store with her head down. She'd gone home and canceled her flight and waited for the pain of missing him to subside—even a little bit.

But it didn't. It was with her when she slept because she could still remember what it was like to feel him sleeping in the bed beside her. And he was with her when she was awake because she could remember what it was like to share a meal across from him at her kitchen table. And laugh with him. And be with him. She shouldn't have ever let him into her home.

Or her heart.

Now she was staring at a black screen wondering what he would say, what he would wear. She hadn't prepped his outfit with him. She'd planned to do it that afternoon, after the breakfast where everything fell apart.

Her tablet chimed and she picked it up off the coffee table. Ben wanted to talk. She accepted the call and saw his face pop on the screen. Even though they talked fairly regularly, she still hadn't gone to see him at his home. She told herself she was following doctor's orders by keeping him completely quarantined except for his nurse, but the truth was it was an effort for her to get out of her bed, let alone her house.

She thought he looked good. Changing a little every day. His hair was completely gone, but his face showed some scruff as if he hadn't shaved. And his cheeks looked fuller as if he was finally starting to put back on some of the weight he'd lost. She wondered if Anna had talked to him yet. She had said they might have to talk eventually and while Madeleine was curious about why, she hadn't pushed. Anna was a lot like Ben in that regard. She was only ever going to tell you what she wanted you to know.

"Hi."

"Are you watching this?"

"No. I'm DVRing it. In case I want to watch it later."

"You should watch."

"Why? What's he saying? Is he off script?" Madeleine's hand reached for the remote control, but still she couldn't make herself push the power button. "How does he look?"

"Like a man who has lost something. You should watch."

"It's too hard," she said, looking away from the tablet to stare at the blank screen.

"Madeleine, you're disappointing me."

That had her head shooting up. "I'm sorry if my grief is bothersome to you."

"It's not your grief that's bothersome. It's your cowardice. I know you to be a brilliant woman. I didn't think you were a fearful one, as well."

It hurt, but could she refute it? Isn't that exactly what she called herself? Weak and frightened. It made her sick. She was more disgusted with herself for being a coward than she was when she'd had sex with the president.

"He's a brave man, Michael Langdon. You could learn something from him."

"You're not helping, Ben."

"This call wasn't meant to help. Madeleine, I hate to be cliché so I can't believe you're making me be the one to tell you this. Life is too short for wasting time. You wasted time before I found you and you're wasting it again. You're not that stupid. Now, turn on the TV and watch from the beginning."

The call ended and Madeleine set the tablet

down. Someday she was going to point out to Ben that he wasn't the best at pep talks.

The blank screen taunted her. What had Michael said? Why did Ben think she needed to watch?

And what had he meant when he said Michael was brave?

The only thing she could do was turn on the TV and watch. Could she be as brave?

CHAPTER NINETEEN

"LET'S TALK ABOUT your past."

They weren't two minutes into the interview and Lynn Connelly, the TV reporter Peg had chosen to do the interview, was already getting to the hard stuff. The first few minutes had been a montage of Michael as a Formula One racer turned businessman. Then when the interview started Lynn had gotten him comfortable by asking some questions about his success as a race-car driver.

Michael looked beautiful to Madeleine. He'd worn a deep blue sweater and dark gray slacks. Nothing flashy that hinted at the playboy he used to be. Instead he was the sound and successful businessman he'd become.

"It's a well-known fact you were arrested at nineteen for car theft and sentenced to three years in a state facility."

"It is."

"You served all three years of your sentence, which seems unusual for a first-time offender. No parole for good behavior?"

It was a leading question. Madeleine could see it in the reporter's eyes. Lynn was waiting for Michael to lie about the events that kept him in jail because she already knew about the assault. *Damn it,* she should have barred this line of questioning. She should have told Peg his past wasn't something that was open for conversation. What did she care if it made him look like he was hiding something? He was selling a car, not himself.

Stupid, so stupid of her, and now he might be walking into a trap.

"I wasn't particularly well behaved."

It was the answer he'd given her once. Such a casual dismissal of everything that had happened to him. Would it be enough for Lynn to accept it and move on? Please let it be enough. Madeleine held her breath.

"The record shows that while you were in prison you were involved in a fight with another inmate."

"I was."

"Michael, you beat this man so severely he was in a coma for a time."

"I did."

Madeleine watched as Michael crossed and uncrossed his legs. *He wants to pace,* she thought. *It's probably killing him that he can't move.*

"Is it something you can talk about?"

"Can or will?"

"Both."

The camera focused in on Michael exclusively and Madeleine could see it in his expression. There was a certain resolve there, like he was staring down the barrel of a gun and choosing not to step away.

She was tempted to turn off the television, but her hands shook as she reached for the remote and then it was too late. He was already talking.

"People hear stories about what happens to some men in prison. People even make jokes about it. Some use these awful stories to scare young punks who don't know any better into going clean. All I can tell you is that some of those stories are real and horrific. I physically assaulted a man in retaliation to an act that was done to me. And while it did cost me two years of my life, I felt it was my only option at the time. And I think that's all I can say about it."

Madeleine choked on a sob. Why? Why would he say it? On television in front of everyone, when she knew how long and how tight he'd held on to his secret.

The screen filled with Lynn's face, which was offering a sympathetic look.

"While I can't condone your actions, I can tell you I think it was certainly brave of you to come forward about it. Why talk about it now? After all this time?"

"I've been holding on to the past for a long time. Or I should say, it's been holding on to me. And when you let something like that control you, it builds these walls between you and everyone around you. I want to be done with it."

"Are you? Done with it?"

"Yeah...I think I am. You might say I'm... cured. What I didn't realize until just this moment was that I had the power over it all this time. I brought my own walls down. Yeah, I didn't know I could do that."

"Okay, well, let's talk about your car..."

The scene broke and Michael and Lynn were walking through what Michael called his Pimp Garage. Craig was there, along with some others from the team. Then Charles Blakely came into the shot and they both began to talk about their partnership and what it meant.

Madeleine stared at the screen, not really seeing or hearing what was happening. Her head was filled with his words. Her heart was filled with his message to her.

Meet the past head-on. But he was so much stronger than she was.

The scene changed again, and it was once more Lynn and Michael sitting in his home.

"Let's talk about your love life."

Madeleine gasped at the question. The picture wouldn't have been out when they'd filmed this. Lynn couldn't know about them as a couple. Which meant it was a run-of-the-mill question. Asking a handsome, successful, well-known playboy if he was finally ready to settle down. What interviewer wouldn't go there?

"Is there anyone special in your life right now?"

Madeleine waited as Michael paused, wondering what he had been thinking.

"Right now? No."

The answer was tight and harsh sounding and it broke her heart all over again. This was either filmed the day she left him or maybe the day after. At the most she had only been gone for three days.

He'd obviously believed her when she'd told him it was over.

"Do you want there to be? A particular someone."

"Desperately."

"And what are you looking for in a woman?"

"What turns me on, you mean?"

"Yes, I suppose. What is your number one must-have?"

It was supposed to be a light moment. A bit of flirting between Lynn and Michael to draw the audience in further. Madeleine waited for his answer like he was about to provide the location of the Holy Grail.

"I really dig...courage in a woman. Might sound crazy, but courage is a hell of a thing."

"Interesting. And finally, tell us what's next for you."

"Congress. Charles and I and some other representatives from the auto industry have been called to speak before a committee about the potential of our car. Together we can look for some new ways to encourage the American people to go green and help the environment...."

Madeleine turned the television off.

Distantly, she considered how well he'd done. He'd been heartbreakingly honest about his past. Nearly boyish with enthusiasm when talking about his car. So much so that it probably removed from people's minds the horror of what prison had been for him, because they could see with their own eyes how he had overcome everything. The man he'd become was simply amazing. And to tie everything up with his message for a better environment? He couldn't have been more impressive.

Hell, if he were ever interested she might have a chance of getting him elected president.

Because that's what she used to do. She used to make presidents.

Looking around her empty house, she thought back to that person. She remembered Pre-Scandal Madeleine very clearly. She was brilliant and ambitious. She took chances no one thought of and saw things no one could. She was aggressive. Some might have said arrogant, but she would have countered those accusations with her own labels: confident and determined.

Yes, PSM was a beast on wheels. A king-maker.

She was fearless.

Now she was gone, trapped behind protective walls of her own making. Everything outside those walls had been taken from her, all her dreams and plans gone before she had been twenty-eight years old.

Courage was something someone needed in a fight. But for Madeleine there could be no battle. No war she could wage against what had happened to her because it had been all her fault. Was she supposed to rail at the horrible names she was being called? Was she supposed to fight back against the paparazzi who stalked her for money, when she knew it was her own actions that had caused them to go after her?

It was seven years ago.... How long do I have to pay?

Seven years ago, yes. But she was still worthy of a seedy picture on the cover of a rag magazine.

Because of Michael. The picture was there because of him...not you.

Her own thoughts were betraying her. Because deep down, she knew what she wanted.

She wanted Michael back. She wanted to be the woman who deserved him. She wanted to be courageous.

"And when you let something like that control you, it builds these walls between you and everyone around you."

He'd said those words to the camera and the world thought he'd been talking about himself.

Madeleine knew otherwise.

"ARE YOU ready?"

Blakely came up behind Michael and slapped him on the back. They were standing in a hallway outside of the congressional meeting hall waiting as the people gathered for the hearing. The halls were abuzz with people, all of whom seemed in a hurry to be somewhere else.

Then Michael spotted some men bringing television cameras and other equipment into the room where they were meeting.

"I thought we were doing this privately."

"Too many people want to see this so we're opening it up and letting some news crews in. Which is good for us. The more publicity, the better. Hell, we're already taking orders for your car and we haven't even rolled the first one off the production line."

Michael's interview had worked like a charm. People got to see the car, and not only that, they were also able to associate it with the American Dream story behind it. Poor kid grows up, suffers horrible attack in prison, but overcomes everything and makes it big in America. People wanted to drive his car for that reason alone. Blakely seemed about to rub his hands together with glee. Michael knew he was thinking about all the money he was going to make. The other executives were kicking themselves for not acting sooner and partnering up with Michael when they'd had the chance.

"What kind of questions are we expecting?"

"Questions that will make the men and women on the committee look good on camera. Remember who we're dealing with here. The only thing most politicians really care about is getting reelected. Besides, you survived Lynn Connelly, how hard could it be to answer their questions?" Blakely gave him another slap on the back. "I'm going inside to get settled. You'll sit on my right when you're ready."

"Yeah, yeah...just give me a minute."

Blakely nodded and opened the twelve-foot-high door into the room. Michael could hear bustling inside from all the people gathering and felt his stomach turn a little. He told himself it wasn't the stupidest thing to be slightly nervous about a congressional hearing. Besides, he was here for a positive reason. It's not like they were going to grill him on steroids or weapon smuggling or something serious like that.

He took a deep breath. This was about his car. That's it. Still, for the hundredth time, he wished he could have at least called Madeleine. She would have told him what to expect. She would have prepared him by describing the political leanings of everyone in the room. She would have told him who cared more about job creation and who cared more about saving the earth.

She would have told him how to focus his answers and say the things the person asking the question most wanted to hear.

But she wasn't here. Hell, just asking her to come had been enough to send her running.

For the hundredth time, he wondered if she had even watched his interview. There had been a brief hope that after she saw it, she might come back. He clung to the memory that, standing at the foot of his stairs, she hadn't been able to tell him that she didn't love him. Which meant that if she did, and if she saw what he did for her, then maybe she could take the next step.

His big gesture.

He thought by confessing everything on television he'd offered her a road map on how to overcome her fears. He'd wanted to show her that holding on to the past was a dead end. The only way to be free of it was to truly meet her past head-on.

But she hadn't come.

Then there was no hope for it. He was left with only two choices. Forget about her and move on with his life or go get her. The answer was simple.

He was going to have to go to her.

Because there was no way he was living without her. This broken-heart stuff was horseshit, in his opinion. He couldn't figure out why country singers reveled in it so much, because he was done with it.

He knew what it was like to live with her, he knew he loved her and damn it, he was pretty sure she loved him, too. If she was too scared to come to him, then fine. He would go to her and he would stay locked in her house with her until she felt safe enough to step outside again.

They would start over and take it slower. Dr. Sheffield had been right about that. He should have gone much slower until Madeleine felt safe. Instead he'd pushed too hard, he'd wanted too much too fast, but now he knew he needed to be more careful with her.

Slow wasn't exactly his favorite speed, but for her he would make it work. He would make anything work.

Having made the decision, he felt good. It was like the dark cloud that had been circling overhead had finally drifted away. As soon as the hearing was over he would take the train to Philadelphia, and if he had to bust down her front door with a sledgehammer to get her to let him in, then he would do it.

He turned to open the door when the sound of heels clicking on marble caught his attention.

Click, click, click.

Slow, even, measured steps. This person wasn't rushing or scurrying anywhere. This person was simply walking with a purpose and with power.

Michael turned his head toward the sound with the faint idea that he might actually be seeing the president himself. But the sound of the click was delicate and Michael figured it was unlikely the current male president would be walking around the halls of Congress in high heels.

He saw her and his heart stopped and his head rang. Exactly like the first time he saw her when he'd felt as if he'd been hit on the head with a bat. Everything other than Madeleine suddenly became fuzzy, and a buzzing noise sounded in his ear.

Her hair was pinned into a tight bun, her chin was still a little too pointy—which made her even more beautiful to him. As she walked, her gray suit hugged her curves: the skirt grazed her knees and her blazer was buttoned up like a woman ready to do battle. His very own warrior in high heels. Who was about to change his life forever.

She saw him and stopped. He could see the concern in her face. Like maybe she'd come too late. She didn't know that it could never be too late. Not for him. Not ever.

Then she lifted her chin a little higher and walked toward him. He considered how brave she was and yes, that really was a turn-on.

"You came," he whispered, having a hard time speaking over the lump in his throat. He'd never felt this way before. Never knew it was conceivable to feel this way. This was happiness. The real thing.

She raised a single eyebrow and he wanted to throw her down on the marble floor and have his way with her.

"You didn't think I would let you go in there without backup. This is my turf and it's a nasty one. You need to know the players, you need to know the agenda. You will want to make sure you are answering the right person in the right way."

"You came," he said again.

She ducked her head then, but he used a finger to lift her face to his because he wanted to see her eyes and know that everything she was about to say was the truth.

"I shouldn't have left. I'm sorry I did. Sorry I ran."

"I forgive you. Now say it."

She swallowed a few times.

"Come on," he urged. "It isn't going to be any harder than walking through the front door of this building."

"Yes, it is. It's much harder, because you mean a hell of a lot more to me than anything I could feel being back here. That's how I knew you were right. That I can face the past because all my shame and guilt and embarrassment…it's nothing when you hold it up to love."

He smiled. "You're right. It isn't. So say it."

"I love you."

He nodded and the strength of those words filled him like nothing had ever done before. "Don't ever run from me again. Please."

"I won't," she said as she moved closer. "Turns out I had courage all along. I just forgot where I put it."

He took a step toward her and wrapped his arm around her back, bringing her closer to his body so they were nearly touching. Tilting his head, he whispered into her ear, "You know, I have this thing for courage. It sort of turns me on."

"I heard. But we have some other pressing matters to attend to first."

"I'd rather do you instead."

She laughed and it warmed his heart.

"I'm sure you would," she said, taking a little nip of his ear. "Word in this town has it I'm a pretty good time, if you know what I mean."

"We'll have to see about that," he said, taking her hand. He reached for the door. "You know there are going to be cameras."

"Yep."

"You know there are going to be gasps when people realize it's you."

"Yep."

"You're shaking," he said, feeling her hands tremble in his.

"I am, but I'm not sure if that's from fear or happiness. Let's go with happiness."

"One last time, are you ready for this?" Michael asked.

"With you beside me…I'm ready for anything."

He smiled as he opened the door and they walked through the throng of cameras together.

* * * * *